FIGHTING FANTASY

BLACK LOBSTER

THE PORT OF PERIL

IAN LIVINGSTONE

Fighting Fantasy: dare you play them all?

And look out for more books to come!

THE PORT OF PERIL

IAN LIVINGSTONE

SCHOLASTIC

MOUNTAINS

Fang RIVER KOK

Zengis

Anvil

Stonebridge Firetop Mountain

KAY-PONG

PLAINS

MOONSTONE HILLS

DARKWOOD FOREST

Yaztromo's Tower

Deedle Water

FOREST OF SPIDERS

RIVER Largo

SILVER RIVER CHALICE

SILVERTON

Coven

KNOTOAK WOOD

TROLLTOOTH PASS

WINDWARD PLAIN

FOREST OF YORE

WATER RIVER

PLAIN

SHAZÂAR

VALE OF WILLOW

SALAMONS

TO THE FLATLANDS

Vatos

Black Tower

CRAGGEN HEIGHTS

LEO HARTAS

Scholastic Children's Books
An imprint of Scholastic Ltd
Euston House, 24 Eversholt Street, London, NW1 1DB, UK
Registered office: Westfield Road, Southam, Warwickshire, CV47 0RA
SCHOLASTIC and associated logos are trademarks and/or
registered trademarks of Scholastic Inc.

First published in the UK by Scholastic Ltd, 2017

ISBN 978 1407 18129 5

A CIP catalogue record for this book
is available from the British Library.

Printed by CPI Group (UK) Ltd, Croydon, CR0 4YY
Papers used by Scholastic Children's Books are made
from wood grown in sustainable forests.

3 5 7 9 10 8 6 4 2

www.scholastic.co.uk

CONTENTS

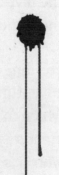

HOW WILL YOU START YOUR ADVENTURE?

The book you hold in your hands is a gateway to another world – a world of dark magic, terrifying monsters, brooding castles, treacherous dungeons and untold danger, where a noble few defend against the myriad schemes of the forces of evil. Welcome to the world of **FIGHTING FANTASY!**

You are about to embark upon a thrilling fantasy adventure in which **YOU** are the hero! **YOU** decide which route to take, which dangers to risk and which creatures to fight. But be warned – it will also be **YOU** who has to live or die by the consequences of your actions.

Take heed, for success is by no means certain, and you may well fail in your mission on your first attempt. But have no fear, for with experience, skill and luck, each new attempt should bring you a step closer to your ultimate goal.

Prepare yourself, for when you turn the page you will enter an exciting, perilous **FIGHTING FANTASY** adventure where every choice is yours to make, an adventure in which **YOU ARE THE HERO!**

How would you like to begin your adventure?

IF YOU ARE NEW TO FIGHTING FANTASY...

It's a good idea to read through the rules which appear on pages 277-283 before you start.

IF YOU HAVE PLAYED FIGHTING FANTASY BEFORE...

You'll realize that to have any chance of success, you will need to discover your hero's attributes. You can create your own character by following the instructions on pages 277–283. Don't forget to enter your character's details on the Adventure Sheet which appears on page 284.

ALTERNATIVE DICE

If you do not have a pair of dice handy, dice rolls are printed throughout the book at the bottom of the pages. Flicking rapidly through the book and stopping on a page will give you a random dice roll. If you need to 'roll' only one die, read only the first printed die; if two, total the two dice symbols.

BACKGROUND

Chalice is an affluent town on the north bank of Silver River, a wide, twisting river which flows gently down from the Moonstone Hills to merge with Catfish River on its way to the Western Ocean. It began as nothing more than a merchant's store built at the end of a wooden jetty used by river traders to land their goods. At first, trade was very slow, and the merchant complained he'd been handed a poisoned chalice. Trade slowly improved, but the name stuck, and over time Chalice grew to become a busy river port.

Chalice's inhabitants are mostly human, and it is also home to a number of other races. There are Elves, who always seem to know more about what's going on than anybody else; Striders, who run around town on their spindly long legs doing errands; Man-Orcs, who are usually hired as guards; Gnomes, who spend most of their time slurping down bowls of pea soup; two beefy Ogres, who hire themselves out to do most of the heavy lifting jobs; and an unusually friendly Cyclops, who arrived one day long ago with goods to trade and never left. He acquired the nickname of Cy, became a blacksmith, and quickly built a reputation as the best smithy in Chalice. He later turned his skills to crafting the finest swords in Northern Allansia, but never made more than one a month, as he refused to compromise on quality. Cy proudly sells his famous 'One Eye' swords for 50 Gold Pieces each. A 'quality price for a quality product,' as he says with gusto to his customers, and he is never short of those.

Commerce is the main reason for Chalice's prosperity. Merchants arrive from all over Allansia to sell their wares in the town, where prices are always at a premium. Vendors pack the market square six days a week selling weapons, armour, potions, lotions, herbs, spices, grain, livestock, semi-precious stones, jewellery, silk, furs, fine textiles and exotic foodstuffs. Money changes hands from dawn till dusk in brisk trading. Although Chalice has its fair share of impoverished folk, it affords nobles, merchants, landlords and innkeepers a fine living. And like any large town with wealthy inhabitants, Chalice also attracts pickpockets and thieves who see the opportunity to relieve some of the more naive townsfolk of their hard-earned silver and gold. Young con artists learn their devious skills in Chalice, spinning yarns and practising their scams on the locals. If they don't get caught, the best of them journey downriver to try their luck on the citizens of Port Blacksand, where they must compete with hardened professional thieves and vagabonds.

YOU are a seasoned adventurer, an experienced sword-for-hire who enjoys slaying monsters and finding treasure above anything else. Despite some memorable adventures, you have learned the hard way that treasure hunting does not always guarantee the reward of glittering gold. More often than not, treasure hunters come back from their expeditions empty-handed. And when things don't go well, adventurers reluctantly have to resort to working for others, usually earning a low wage guarding rich nobles' estates or protecting merchants' caravans on their journeys to market. You recently arrived in Chalice tired and hungry after spending a month scouring the Pagan Plains trying, but failing, to find the buried treasure hoard of Throm, the notorious axe-wielding barbarian who, rumour has it, died in Baron Sukhumvit's infamous Deathtrap Dungeon in Fang trying to win the grand prize of 10,000 Gold Pieces.

Your days spent in Chalice have been anything but enjoyable. Unable to find work, you are forced to sleep rough in alleyways, scavenging for scraps of food left

Two men stagger outside arm in arm

abandoned by traders in the market square at the end of the day. It is a warm evening on day four of your stay. The sun is slowly sinking in the western sky and the light is beginning to fade. You are standing outside the Fat Frog Inn drooling over the menu nailed to the oak door when two men stagger outside arm in arm. One is middle-aged, bearded, and wearing a brown leather tunic over dark green leggings, whilst the younger one is wearing a checked woollen shirt tucked into his baggy brown pants. Both men are giggling like children, very much the worse for the amount of ale they have drunk. They brush past you, oblivious to everything. The younger man is hiccuping and swaying erratically from side to side. He tries to grab hold of the back of a wooden bench to steady himself, but misses it, and falls over, cursing. This causes his friend to laugh even louder. The younger man sits up, squinting in the bright light, his mouth hanging open like a gormless fool.

'Eryk!' the younger man splutters, hiccuping.

'What?'

'Stop laughing at me.'

'Why?'

'Because I'm going to be rich!'

'Shut up,' the older man replies dismissively.

'I am! I'm going to be rich! I bought a treasure map!' he retorts, reaching into his pocket to produce an old piece of parchment as evidence. Too drunk to notice that he's holding it upside down, he stares at it with a befuddled expression on his face. Although you're well within earshot, you pretend not to be listening.

'How much did you pay for it?'

'Four Copper Pieces.'

'Four Copper Pieces? What a fool you are. There's not a hope that it's genuine. You've been done, Gregor,' the older man says, laughing even louder. 'Stitched up like a kipper. A fool chasing fool's gold, that's what you are. You just don't learn, do you? You can't believe anything anyone says in the Fat Frog Inn.'

'But... But that old man seemed so genuine. He had an honest face, unlike all those other sharks and villains in there giving it large. I wanted to believe him. I did believe him!'

'Are you going to go back in to get your money back?'

'Nah, the poor man needed the money. He sounded desperate. I felt sorry for him. That's why I bought the map really. No hard feelings. I enjoyed listening to his tale about the iron chest filled with golden amulets. He said it was hidden deep inside a cave in Moonstone Hills. And he kept going on about a gold ring in the chest. Said it was more valuable than all the amulets put together. What did he call it again? The Ring of. . . Oh, fiddle! I can't remember now. But it doesn't matter if it isn't true! Or you say it isn't true. Or whatever.'

'Forget about it, Gregor. He made it all up.'

'The Ring of Burning Snakes! That's what he called it. He said it used to belong to an old wizard called Nico or Nico something or other. He said the wizard would pay a pretty penny to get it back.'

'I said forget about it, Gregor. Come on, get up, let's try the Sun Inn next. I'm thirsty!' Eryk says sternly, pulling his friend up off the ground.

'All right, all right. I won't be needing this, then!' Gregor says, crumpling up the parchment into a ball and tossing it over his shoulder before staggering off.

The parchment ball lands just by your feet. Intrigued, you bend down to pick it up. You unfold it to reveal a very detailed hand-drawn map of the land surrounding Chalice.

The map shows a dotted line heading north from Chalice, then east, some way south of Darkwood Forest, crossing the Eastern Plain to Moonstone Hills, where a large *X* marks the entrance to a cave in Skull Crag, one of the highest peaks in the range. There is a message in tiny handwriting written in black ink on the back of the map which says, *Do NOT enter by the cave entrance. Climb the crag to a ledge twenty metres above. Move the standing branches aside to reveal the secret entrance. Enter here and turn left, right, right at the junctions. An iron chest will be found in the Crystal Cave. Good luck! Murgat Shurr.*

Could a treasure chest really lie hidden in a cave inside Skull Crag? Why would an old man sell his secrets for a few Copper Pieces? And who is Murgat Shurr? Nothing makes sense. You are about to toss the map away when you hear the shrill squawk of a bird overhead. You look up to see a crow flying north. Could it be an omen? Could this be your lucky day after all? You decide you have nothing to lose and everything to gain. You fold up the parchment and put it safely away in your pocket. Tomorrow you will set off for Skull Crag. But right now you need to find some food and somewhere to sleep before nightfall.

NOW TURN OVER . . .

YOUR
ADVENTURE
AWAITS!

MAY YOUR STAMINA NEVER FAIL!

You fail to find any food, and resign yourself to sleeping on some old flour sacks left outside a baker's shop at the end of an alley. You place your blanket on top of the sacks and lie down as darkness falls, ending the day exhausted and very hungry. You hear a dog sniffing nearby, but eventually fall asleep, dreaming of treasure chests overflowing with Gold Pieces and diamonds.

Reality returns early the following morning when you are rudely woken not long after sunrise by the sound of cockerels crowing loudly. The air is chill, but the skies are clear – at least another fine day is in store. You grab your trusty sword, roll up your blanket and check the few belongings you have in your backpack. They don't amount to much: a **ball of twine**, a **candle**, a **small brass bell**, an **oil lantern**, a **knife**, a **piece of chalk**, a **brass owl**, a **length of rope**, a **bag of copper nails**, an **animal-skin water flask** and a **goblet bearing a unicorn-head motif**. You make your way to the town square and fill your flask with water which flows from the spout of a fountain carved in the shape of a dragon's head. After quenching your thirst, you search through a pile of rubbish and find some squashed tomatoes and a chunk of bread left to rot in a wooden crate. The bread is stale but right now a tomato sandwich seems like the breakfast of champions. Add 1 *STAMINA* point. The sandwich takes the edge off your hunger but you know you could eat more. There is nobody about except for a tall, middle-aged man with curly brown hair who is whistling happily to himself as he sweeps the square with a long broom. A leather shoulder bag is slung over his back. If you want to talk to him, turn to **19**. If you would rather leave the market square, turn to **58**.

2

You are soon back at the fork in the path. 'Going left will takes us south and out of the forest. We need to go straight on here to reach Yaztromo's Tower,' Hakasan says without stopping. Turn to **252**.

3

The arrows fly past you, lodging harmlessly into trees. You jump up and charge the Bandits before they have time to reload, swinging your sword in the air. Fight them one at a time.

	SKILL	STAMINA
First BANDIT	6	7
Second BANDIT	7	7
Third BANDIT	7	6

If you win, turn to **22**.

4

As if things couldn't get any worse, you are now without your trusty sword. The sword you get in exchange is old and fairly blunt. Lose 1 *LUCK* point and 2 *SKILL* points. You are angry with yourself for thinking you could beat the card sharp and decide to leave the market square. Turn to **58**.

5

You offer the Trolls 1 Gold Piece each to let you enter the palace gardens. Twoteeth laughs out loud. 'Two Gold Pieces?' he says, scoffing at your offer. 'Do you think that we would risk Lord Azzur's wrath for 2 Gold Pieces? We want 10 Gold Pieces each, nothing less.' If you have 20 Gold Pieces and want to pay the Trolls, turn to **145**. If you can't pay or won't pay, your only choice is to let them take your weapons and look inside your backpack. Turn to **192**.

You reach into your pocket and unfold the yellow handkerchief. Nicodemus's jaw drops in disbelief as he picks up the large gold ring on display in the palm of your hand. 'The Ring of Burning Snakes!' he says ecstatically. 'Where did you find it?' You tell him that it's a long story, but he insists on hearing every bit of it, from the moment you picked up Murgat Shurr's map in Chalice to rescuing him from the cells. You finish the tale just as you reach the jetty in Flax. You wave to Dod, who is standing nearby, tying up piles of reeds into bundles, ready to carry them home. He walks over to help you tie up the boat, saying, 'Welcome back. I hope you found what you looking for in that cesspit of a town. Thank you for bringing my boat back. It looks quite a bit bigger than I remember! It's changed colour too.' You apologize and explain what happened, and introduce him to Nicodemus and Luannah. Dod is very happy with his new boat and invites you into his house, where Cris is frying fish. She invites you to stay for supper, and suggests you stay the night too since it's getting late. You accept her offer and wake early in the morning to find Cris and Luannah deep in conversation. Luannah announces that she has decided to stay in Flax to start a new life, and you wish her all the best. Dod brings Stormheart round to the front of the house, and you help Nicodemus mount the horse before climbing on yourself. A light flick of the reins, and Stormheart gallops off at high speed. You look round briefly to see the three of them waving, but you kick on knowing there is no time to lose. Galloping towards Largo, you see a man in a scruffy brown jacket and ragged britches trudging slowly along with the aid of a long walking stick, weighed down by an enormous bulging sack. On hearing the sound of the galloping hooves behind him, he turns around and waves at you with his woollen hat, signalling for you to stop. If you want to stop to talk to him, turn to **93**. If you would rather not waste any time, and ride on to Darkwood Forest, turn to **286**.

7

Onx looks you in the eye, and says, 'Before you go, tell me, why did you run after me and then decide not to buy my Healing Potion after all?' You reply, saying that 4 Gold Pieces is too much to pay, especially since he cursed you. 'So I'll meet you halfway, then. How about 3 Gold Pieces for the potion?' If you want to buy the Healing Potion for 3 Gold Pieces, turn to **277**. If you think it is still too much to pay for a potion and would rather set off for Darkwood Forest, turn to **47**.

8

Armoury Lane is only a hundred metres long, but every building in it has been turned into an armourer's shop. All the shop windows are protected by thick iron grills to stop anybody breaking in and helping themselves to all the weapons and armour on display. There are swords, cleavers, spears, picks, pikes, axes and poleaxes, clubs, maces, war hammers, helmets, body armour and shields of every shape and size on display. All the shops are closed bar one which has a door almost twice the height of the other doors in the street. There is an open sign on the iron-battened oak door. A small sign in the window reads *We have your size at Cy's.* You peer through the window but do not see anybody inside. If you want to go in the shop, turn to **384**. If you would rather walk to the end of Armoury Lane, turn to **33**.

9

Onx looks at you with an annoyed expression on his face, saying, 'Suit yourself,' before walking off, shaking his head. You leave Largo and set off east towards

Darkwood Forest, wondering whether or not you will get back to Hakasan before nightfall. As you walk along through the tall grasses, you do not realize that you have walked into a patch of Weedleweed, a tall grass that is home to TICK-TICKS, tiny parasitic mites which not only suck their host's blood, but infect them with a virus which makes them very sleepy. You start to yawn uncontrollably, and have no choice but to lie down and go to sleep. *Test Your Luck*. If you are lucky, turn to **160**. If you are Unlucky, turn to **96**.

10

If you have more than one bottle in your possession, you will have to choose which one to use. If you want to use the potion from the green bottle, turn to **172**. If you want to use the potion from the brown bottle, turn to **158**.

Its mouth opens to reveal two rows of flesh-ripping teeth

11

The unholy beast strides forward with heavy steps which makes the ground tremble. It is grey-green in colour with ugly red veins protruding from its skin. It has giant-sized clawed hands with suckered palms, but the most terrifying thing is its enormous mouth, which is almost as wide as its torso. Its mouth opens to reveal two rows of flesh-ripping teeth, and six long, suckered tentacles which shoot out from its throat, flailing around in the air. The vile beast is QUAG-SHUGGUTH, a Lesser Demon summoned from the Plain of Pain by Zanbar Bone. It has tiny eyes and is virtually blind, but it senses your presence and knows exactly where you are. You have no choice but to fight it! If you own a Venom Sword, turn to **337**. If you do not own this sword, turn to **202**.

12

There are five houses in a row, all of them grand and in very good order, no doubt owned by some of the rich merchants of Chalice. You hear the noise of a window sliding open above you, and look up to see a woman with long curly red hair lean out and yell at you not to look in her windows. 'Go away!' she screams in a rage, and throws a chamber pot down at you. *Test Your Luck*. If you are Lucky, turn to **271**. If you are Unlucky, turn to **153**.

13

The youngest beggar snatches the map from you and examines it carefully. 'I'll tell you what I know about this map for another Copper Piece!' he says, looking closely at the tiny writing. You agree to pay him, although you're a little annoyed at his cheek. He pockets the coin and declares, 'The writing is in black ink and the treasure is located with a large *X*. It must be genuine!' You thank the man for his opinion, but have a feeling he was just making it up. You decide against starting an argument and bid the beggars farewell. Turn to **311**.

14

You follow Yaztromo down two flights of stairs to his cluttered kitchen area, where pots and pans are bubbling away on top of a large iron stove. 'I hope you like mushroom soup and vegetable stew,' he says brightly, lifting the lids off the saucepans to sniff the rich aromas wafting up. 'Delicious. Simply delicious,' he continues. 'I might have some cheese and biscuits to follow if you are still hungry. Please, sit down, and I will serve the soup.' You sit down at his oval dining table with Hakasan to enjoy Yaztromo's food, and both agree it is the most delicious meal either of you have had in as long as you can remember. Add 2 *STAMINA* points. You talk about Zanbar Bone long into the night with Yaztromo, who later has a nightcap of his favourite sherry to accompany the last of his cream cakes, which he enthuses about down to the last crumb. He shows you to your bedrooms and, being slightly tipsy, wishes you goodnight, laughing out loud in an uncharacteristically jovial fashion. You have vivid dreams of skeletons and demons, and wake up in a cold sweat in the middle of the night. You look out of your bedroom window at the starlit night sky and the endless treetops of Darkwood Forest. All is quiet and peaceful. You eventually fall asleep again and wake up late. You are the last one down for breakfast, and find Hakasan and Yaztromo deep in conversation at the table. 'Morning!' Yaztromo says, smiling. 'I trust you slept well? After breakfast I think it best that you go to Port Blacksand by yourself. Firstly, Hakasan needs more rest. Her ankle is swollen again. Secondly, I only have one horse! The sooner you get to Port Blacksand and find Nicodemus, the sooner you will be back. But before you go, I think a little magic is in order to help you out! I can offer you improved fighting ability, increased strength or good fortune. Eat your breakfast whilst you decide what you need.' Will you:

Improve your *SKILL*?	Turn to **215**
Improve your *STAMINA*?	Turn to **78**
Improve your *LUCK*?	Turn to **288**

15

You look around the small room, hoping to find something you could use to help you escape, but there is nothing. You resign yourself to being locked away for six months. The first days drag by slowly, your only contact with the outside world coming when the jailer arrives once a day with his basket of maggot-infested bread and a jug of water. As the weeks pass, you lose weight and become too tired to even fend off the rats which creep through the window at night to eat the crumbs on the floor. You suffer several bites from the rats and catch a deadly plague. Your adventure is over.

16

The dice players see you looking at them, and beckon you over to sit down at their table. You ask them what game they are playing. 'We're enjoying a little game of Dungles and Draggles,' the bearded player replies jovially. 'It was invented by a Bard called Yog. It's very simple. I roll two dice and add the numbers together. That's my Dungle score. Then you roll two dice for your Draggle score. But before you roll, you have to say if your Draggle score will be higher or lower than my Dungle score. If you guess right, you win. If you guess wrong, you lose. You also lose if you roll the same number. I'm willing to wager my pirate's flintlock pistol for a ruby. Do you want to play?' If you possess a ruby and want to play, turn to **269**. If you would rather go back to the bar, turn to **89**.

17

The Norgul is a powerful creature which fights with brute strength and savage aggression. Dropping the jar of eyeballs on to the ground sends it into a rage, and it launches a frenzied attack on you with flailing fists. It is now eager to feast on your eyes. Its thick hide is not easy to pierce, even with your sharp-edged sword.

NORGUL   SKILL 10   STAMINA 9

If you win, turn to **231**.

18

Onx thanks you for helping him out. When you are back in Largo, he gives you a bottle of healing potion in exchange for 2 Gold Pieces. As a thank-you, he also gives you some fresh fish to eat and a cup of goat's milk to drink. Add 2 *STAMINA* points. Since there are no more boats for hire to take you to Port Blacksand until tomorrow, you decide to go back to Darkwood Forest without further delay. You are about to leave when Onx asks if you would like to buy a pair of bone dice that are handmade by the elders of the village. He tells you that they will bring you luck in any game of dice, and are a bargain at 2 Gold Pieces for the two. If you want to buy the dice, turn to **73**. If you would rather politely refuse, turn to **110**.

19

You call out to the street sweeper, but he ignores you, and carries on whistling to himself while he works. If you want to ask him if he has any food to trade for an item in your backpack, turn to **126**. If you would rather leave the market square, turn to **58**.

20

Mungo slides off his stool, throws 3 Copper Pieces on to the bar to pay for his ale and walks out of the tavern. You follow him outside, and walk along Harbour Wharf past a pirate ship called the *Flying Toucan* to where the *Blue Marlin* is moored. A rough-looking man in black trousers and a hooped top is sitting on the boat whittling a stick. 'I'm pleased to see that you are still here,' Mungo says to him, jumping aboard. He gives the man 5 Copper Pieces and ushers him off the boat before welcoming you on board. He checks the sails and supplies, and tells you to untie the boat from the quay. You cast off, and are quickly under way. There is a good breeze, and the wooden sailing boat cuts through the water with ease, its rigging creaking under the strain. Standing on the bow of the *Blue Marlin*, you look back towards Port Blacksand, which is soon no more than a speck on the coastline. Your mind begins to drift, and you think about Yaztromo and Hakasan, hoping they are safe and wondering when you will see them again. An hour later the sea starts to get choppy as dark clouds gather overhead. A few drops of rain begin to fall, and the waves build as the wind increases. It is not long before the *Blue Marlin* is being battered by a howling gale with waves crashing over the deck. Rain lashes down, and you have to hang on to the rigging for your life as the boat is tossed about on the churning sea. 'We're going to turn around and sail back to Port Blacksand,' Mungo screams in your ear, although you can barely hear him. *Test Your Luck*. If you are Lucky, turn to **327**. If you are Unlucky, turn to **386**.

21

You rummage around inside your backpack to find the pouch, and hurriedly pour the salt out into the palm of your hand. You hurl it at the Giant Lavaworm bearing down on you and watch it thrash about trying to shake off the granules. But the salt sticks to its slimy skin, and the worm's gelatinous flesh begins to melt like butter in a heated pan. Soon there is nothing left on the floor apart from its innards and entrails lying in a pool of green slime. Turn to **382**.

22

You look round and are relieved to see that Hakasan has defeated the other three Bandits. Turn to **372**.

23

The bakers look at each other and shrug before lifting you up. Standing on the shoulders of the taller man, you are just able to grab hold of the top of the wall and pull yourself up. Sitting on top of the wall, you look back down and thank the bakers for helping you. They stare at you with bemused expressions on their faces and walk off, shaking their heads. Looking at Hog House fills you with a sense of foreboding. Its dark stone walls and narrow windows are anything but welcoming. The bakers obviously had good reason to question your motive for climbing over the wall. Suddenly two large, slavering ATTACK DOGS come bounding up to the foot of the wall, barking loudly. If you want to jump down to fight them, turn to **373**. If you would rather jump back down on to the street, turn to **234**.

24

You are not far from the wicker basket when you hear a familiar loud squawk overhead. You look up to see the Warhawk swooping down to attack. You must fight the giant predatory bird, which has returned to pick up the basket. With Hakasan fighting by your side, you are able to attack twice during each Attack Round.

WARHAWK   SKILL 8   STAMINA 8

If you win, turn to **367**.

25

Singing Bridge leads into Bridge Street. You run past its ramshackle houses as fast as you can, and on into the market square. The market is a place of hustle and bustle, with vendors shouting out their special offers in the hope of attracting the last customers of the day. You dash through the crowd, looking from person to person, but see no sign of the guards or Nicodemus. A young urchin runs up to you and says, 'Hey! Who are you looking for?' You ask if he saw an old man being marched through the market square by two guards a few minutes ago. The boy smiles and nods his head, saying, 'I'll tell you which way they went if you pay me 1 Gold Piece!' There are five streets leading out of the square, any one of which the guards could have gone down. If you want to pay 1 Gold Piece for the urchin's information, turn to **211**. If you want to decide for yourself which street to go down, turn to **178**.

26

The old man drops 4 Copper Pieces into your hand as a token of his gratitude. You thank him and walk off. If you want to look around the market, turn to **247**. If you would rather leave the market square, turn to **58**.

27

You rub your chin whilst thinking about what items you might need. Bignose looks at your hand and says, 'The gold ring on your middle finger – can I ask you where you got it from? It looks like the Rune Ring that belonged to my old friend Morri Silverheart, who lost it whilst hunting in Darkwood Forest. Sadly he was later killed by Hill Trolls on the Pagan Plains. Is there anything I could offer you in exchange for it? It would give me great pleasure to return it to his widow.' Hakasan points at a silver pendant in the shape of a dragonfly hanging on a silver chain around Bignose's neck. 'What's that?' she asks. 'It's just a pendant. It's nothing special as far as I know,' Bignose replies. If you want to offer the Rune Ring in exchange for the pendant, turn to **256**. If you want to tell Bignose that you don't want to trade the Rune Ring, turn to **173**.

28

Passing the lifeless Gronks and the Skeleton, you arrive at another junction. If you want to go right, turn to **347**. If you want to go straight on, turn to **316**.

29

Gurnard Jaggle shakes his head and says, 'Do you think you can just enter my house uninvited and leave again as though nothing has happened? Have you forgotten that you are trespassers? Either pay me 1 Gold Piece to leave or suffer the consequences.' If you want to pay 1 Gold Piece to leave Gurnard Jaggle's tree house, turn to **335**. If you would rather attack him, turn to **306**.

30

You see two guards walking along the perimeter wall, and wait until they have gone before making your way to the main entrance gates at the end of the gravel path. There are two guards on duty and you have no choice but to walk past them. Trying to act normal, you get within five metres of them before they challenge you. You decide to run for it, and charge past them as fast as you can. One of the guards gives chase but you are able to lose him running through the back streets. When you think the coast is clear, you make your way to the main town gates and saunter through, whistling happily to yourself. Turn to **64**.

The Troll grunts and says, 'Nobody told me you were coming. But I'm always the last one to find out about things down here. You better follow me.' You walk down the steps to a cold and gloomy corridor which is lit by oil lamps suspended from the ceiling. The Troll lumbers along ahead of you, its huge head almost touching the ceiling, forcing it to duck under the oil lamps. It turns left at a junction in the corridor, soon passing a wooden door on the right which it points at, saying, 'The torture chamber is in there. Wait here and I'll get the old wizard for you from his cell. He's still semi-unconscious from the sleeping potion that was put in his drinking water, so don't expect him to say too much!' The Troll starts laughing, and you seize the opportunity to attack it whilst he is off guard, automatically winning the first Attack Round.

IMPERIAL GUARD TROLL   *SKILL 11*   *STAMINA 11*

If you win, turn to **322**.

Dropping the coin in the box triggers cogs and winches to pull ropes through creaking pulleys to tighten a section of the flooring in the middle of the bridge. Wary of hidden traps, you dismount and lead Stormheart slowly on foot across the narrow bridge to the north side of the river, happily without incident. After feeding and watering your steed, you set off west again at a gallop, with the high city wall surrounding Port Blacksand just visible in the distance. The closer you get, the more you see of the dark rooftops and stark buildings jutting above the wall. You arrive an hour later at a small village of no more than a dozen thatch-roofed cottages just east of Port Blacksand. You are greeted by a smiling lady standing on her porch in front of a stack of wicker baskets. She is wearing a brightly coloured headscarf and a white apron over her long dress. 'Welcome to Flax,' she says in a jolly voice. 'My name's Cris. How can I help you?' You reply by saying you are on your way to Port Blacksand, whereupon her eyebrows rise in mild surprise. 'The thieves there will be pleased to see you. They love taking money from people of your ilk, all la-di-da on your big horse! If I were you, I'd hire a boat from my husband and row downriver and slip into Port Blacksand unnoticed. We can look after your horse while you're gone.' If you want to hire a boat to row to Port Blacksand, turn to **41**. If you want to turn down her offer and ride to the main city gates on Stormheart, turn to **264**.

33

There is a timber yard at the end of Armoury Lane where you see a stocky OGRE in a grubby shirt and brown cropped pants loading oak beams on to shelves, while a man in a black jacket counts the number of beams on each shelf. The yard is formed by tall buildings backing on to each other on three sides, and the only way in and out is via Armoury Lane. The man turns to you and says, 'What can I do for you?' If you want to talk to him, turn to **334**. If you would rather go back to the market square to walk down Beggar's Alley, turn to **283**.

34

You raise your arm and are about to bring your sword crashing down on the fungus-like creature when you hear Hakasan scream, 'Don't do it!' She runs through the clearing holding her hand over her mouth. If you want to ignore her advice and slice open the Sporeball, turn to **397**. If you want to follow her and run through the clearing holding your breath, turn to **232**.

35

The paste tastes so disgusting that you spit it out through the trapdoor on to the ground below. It is not long before your mouth goes completely numb, making it almost impossible to swallow, and you feel a burning sensation in your stomach. Lose 2 *STAMINA* points. You drink lots of water and the burning eventually subsides. If you want to rub a small amount of paste on to a wound, turn to **103**. If you would rather take the jar and bandage back to Hakasan, turn to **325**.

36

With Stormheart back under control, you spur him on towards the wall of Skeletons. You ride into them, sending many of them flying in a flurry of broken bones. Alas, there are just too many of them, and you are unable break through to the front. The Skeletons close in on you, dragging you from your saddle, and not even the magic powers of Nicodemus can hold back the tide of undead. You feel the cold steel of the swords and spears pierce your flesh, and you soon fall unconscious. Your adventure is over.

37

You climb up the steps slowly, sword in hand, and enter the giant mouth, which is damp and has a musty smell. When your eyes adjust to the semi-darkness, you notice a skeleton on the floor. It is holding a sword and is clothed in leather armour. Long black worms are writhing in and out of its eye sockets and mouth. A small wooden box lies in pieces on the floor nearby the skeleton. You pick up the box lid and see it has a beetle motif in its centre. You also find a broken glass vial and a small lead ball, which you put in your pocket.

'Another one of Gurnard's specials!' Hakasan says with a sigh. There is a bronze-studded winged helmet lying on the floor which looks to be your size. If you want to try on the helmet, turn to **392**. If you would rather leave the idol to continue your quest to find Yaztromo, turn to **284**.

38

You pick up a long knife that was lying on the ground and tuck it into your belt. With your sword in hand, you enter the cabin ready for any unexpected surprises. The cabin is very basic. There are three rickety wooden beds lined up against one wall, and a table with three chairs set against the opposite wall. At the far end of the cabin there is an iron cauldron bubbling away on top of a log fire burning in the hearth. The blue liquid is obviously the dye the old man was talking about. There are some cooking utensils and small jars of dried herbs, spices and liquids on a shelf, but little else of interest. If you want to look at the labels on the jars, turn to **330**. If you would rather leave the cabin and carry on to Moonstone Hills, turn to **134**.

39

Finbar asks to look at your pistol. You hand it to him, telling him how you came to be its owner. He looks down the barrel and inspects the flintlock mechanism, saying, 'It's old and needs a good clean, but I've seen worse. The flint needs replacing or it won't fire. I usually charge 2 Gold

Pieces to service a pistol. But I'll give you a good deal. Buy a pouch of black powder for 2 Gold Pieces and I'll service your pistol for 1 Gold Piece.' If you want to pay 3 Gold Pieces, turn to **282**. If you would rather leave the shop and walk to Singing Bridge, turn to **118**.

40

The man smiles, turning over the card to reveal a jack of clubs. 'Hard luck, stranger,' he says hollowly. 'I'm afraid you failed to find the lady. Your sword, please.' If you want to hand over your sword, turn to **4**. If you want to ask him to turn over the queen of spades card before handing over your sword, turn to **155**.

41

You jump down from Stormheart and ask Cris to take you to meet her husband. You find him gathering reeds on the riverbank. He smiles and introduces himself as Dod. You tell him you want to hire a boat, and he looks at you, rubbing his chin, relishing the opportunity to earn some money. 'You'll need a cover story as well as a boat, and I'd suggest you buy a merchant's pass and six of my wife's baskets. You can hire my rowing boat for 5 Gold Pieces, and I'll include the pass and the baskets for 10 Gold Pieces if you're interested?' If you want to hire Dod's rowing boat for 5 Gold Pieces, turn to **54**. If you want to hire his rowing boat, merchant's pass and six wicker baskets for 10 Gold

Pieces, turn to **180**. If you want to turn down his offer and ride to the main city gates on Stormheart, turn to **264**.

42

The Norgul comes to a halt, caught in two minds as to whether to attack you or not. You seize the opportunity to bargain with it. If you want to tell the creature that you will give it the jar of eyeballs if it lets you pass through its lair, turn to **253**. If you want to tell the Norgul that you will give it the jar of eyeballs if it gives you something in exchange and also lets you pass through its lair, turn to **90**.

43

Gurnard gives you some bread, dried meats and hard-boiled eggs for your journey. Add 2 *STAMINA* points. You tell him he should go and retrieve all the deadly wooden boxes he hid in the caves. He nods solemnly, promising to set off right away, adding, 'I'll start with Firetop Mountain. I put three or four in there.' Once outside, you shake hands with the old man and wish him well, telling him that once he has collected the boxes, he should go back to Chalice to see his brother, Jethro. He thanks you for helping him come to his senses, saying, 'I can't thank you enough, my friend. Here, please take my brass compass. It might come in useful should you get lost in the forest. And whilst I cannot give you the Ring of

Burning Snakes, please accept this Rune Ring.' He gives you a gold ring encircled with black enamel runes which you put on your middle finger. He sets off north, soon disappearing from view into the trees. Hakasan surveys the undergrowth, looking for telltale signs of the Chaos Warrior. 'He went south,' she says confidently, pointing at a large footprint in the ground. 'Maybe he's on his way to Chalice to take a riverboat to Port Blacksand to assassinate Nicodemus? That would make Zanbar Bone invincible. There is no time to lose. Chaos Warriors wear heavy armour, so he won't be moving too quickly. We have to catch him before he gets to Chalice. Come on, let's go.' Hakasan sets off running through the trees, following the trail of the Chaos Warrior, occasionally stopping to hack through the dense foliage with her sword. She is in such a hurry to catch up with Klash that she does not see a bear trap in front of her, a deep pit that is covered with sticks and leaves to hide it from view. She falls headlong into the trap, landing heavily at the bottom. You throw your rope down to pull her up, but you can see from the expression on her face that she is quite badly hurt. 'It's my ankle,' she says, grimacing. 'I think it might be broken. You'll have to go on without me. Come back and get me after you have dealt with Klash. I'll be fine.' If you want to keep going after Klash, turn to **156**. If you want to go back to Gurnard Jaggle's tree house to find something to fix up Hakasan's ankle, turn to **258**.

The bald man looks you up and down

The bald man looks you up and down and says, 'You have some nerve walking into the grounds of Hog House without an invite. Lady Francesca de la Vette does not take kindly to intruders. For your information, we are not hiring guards at the moment. If you would care to wait, there might be a vacancy in six months.' Without warning, he shouts, 'Guards!' Suddenly you hear shouting voices and the crunching sound of heavy boots on gravel coming your way. You are soon surrounded by six heavily armed guards, their long spears pointed at you. You are forced to surrender your sword and all your coins to them, and are taken away to be locked inside a dingy, cold cell with bare stone walls in the basement of Hog House. The only light comes through a small barred window high up and out of reach on the north-facing wall. You are told by the Man-Orc jailer that you must survive on a diet of bread and water for the next six months. You slump down on your straw mattress, wondering what to do. If you have an iron key, turn to **294**. If you do not have a key, turn to **15**.

45

As you unsheathe your dagger, a Skeleton breaks through and stabs you in the arm. Lose 1 *SKILL* point and 2 *STAMINA* points. Hakasan cuts the arm off the Skeleton, giving you just enough time to act. Holding the dagger in front of you by the tip of its blade, you take careful aim at Zanbar Bone, with Hakasan screaming at you to hurry. You throw your dagger at the Demon, and watch it fly towards its skull. Roll 1 die and add 1 to the number rolled if your current *SKILL* is 10 or higher. If the total is 1–5, turn to **222**. If the number is 6 or 7, turn to **267**.

46

You walk no more than fifty metres along the narrow tunnel when suddenly you hear a dull rumbling sound coming from behind you. Turn to **157**.

47

Onx walks away, shaking his head in disbelief and muttering to himself. He turns to face you one last time, shakes his fist and shouts, 'You'll be sorry!' You set off east towards Darkwood Forest, wondering whether or not you will get back to Hakasan before nightfall. As you walk along through the tall grasses, you do not realize that you have walked into a patch of Weedleweed, a tall grass that is home to TICK-TICKS, tiny parasitic mites which not only suck their host's blood but infect them with a virus which makes them very sleepy. You start to yawn uncontrollably, and have no choice but to lie down and go to sleep. *Test Your Luck*. If you are Lucky, turn to **160**. If you are Unlucky, turn to **96**.

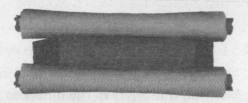

48

You react quickly, grabbing hold of the rat before it can bite you, and smash its head against the barrel, killing it instantly. The other rat scurries off into the shadows. You peer into the barrel but there is nothing inside except for rain-soaked old rags and the rotting carcass of a dead dog. The smell is unbearable. If you want to knock on the front door of the house, turn to **349**. If you would rather walk on to the T-junction, turn to **206**.

49

Somehow you avoid getting any of the deadly acidic sap on you. You watch it pumping out of the vine, causing a foul-smelling cloud of vapour to rise from the ground, hissing like gas. It makes you cough, and you decide to follow Nicodemus into the tower, where Hakasan slams the door shut behind you. Turn to **279**.

50

You look round to see that Hakasan has defeated a second bandit. If there are any bandits left alive, they take flight and disappear into the forest. Turn to **372**.

51

You find 5 Gold Pieces and a locket of grey hair in the clay pot, no doubt from the head of the blind hag. You must decide if you want to take the locket of hair as well as the Gold Pieces before leaving the cave to make your way to Skull Crag. Turn to **236**.

52

Unluckily for you, one of the pirates sees you surface and yells at his fellow crew to row over to you. The pirate boat is alongside you in seconds, and the oarsmen start plunging their oars into the water to strike you. You are caught on the side of the head by one of the oars, which knocks you out. The pirates grab hold of you and haul you into their boat. You wake up to find that they have taken all of your possessions, including your sword. They chain your ankle to the bench seat in the boat and give you an oar. 'Welcome aboard,' says the sneering captain in his black waistcoat with shiny brass buttons. 'You are now officially under the command of Captain Crow. Row hard for the next six months and you might get some of your possessions back.' You try to convince the captain about the imminent return of Zanbar Bone, but he tells you to stop making up fanciful stories and concentrate on rowing. Wondering about the fate of poor Hakasan, you begin your new life as a river pirate. Your adventure is over.

53

The bald man sneers and says, 'So, you are here to collect a letter, are you? That's very interesting. You don't look like a Strider to me. And Lady Francesca de la Vette instructed me only to use Striders for deliveries to and from Hog House. Be off with you or I'll call the guards.' If you want to change your story and say that you are an adventurer down on your luck who is looking for work as a guard, turn to **44**. If you would rather leave Hog House while you have the chance to do so, turn to **30**.

54

You hand 5 Gold Pieces to Cris and step into the small rowing boat. Dod pushes the boat out into the river, saying, 'Moor up at Lobster Wharf. It's very crowded there and nobody will be bothered about you. But don't come back here without my boat. Remember I've got your horse! No boat, no horse. Do we have an understanding?' You nod your head in agreement, smiling, and wave goodbye, reminding Cris to feed and water Stormheart whilst you're away. Turn to **395**.

A gigantic predatory bird flying west

55

The arrows hit the boulder you are hiding behind, bouncing off harmlessly to land on the ground. The Wild Hill Men fire their remaining arrows at you, but they all miss. They shout down, shaking their fists angrily at you. One of them begins throwing rocks and anything to hand out of frustration, including his shoulder bag and bow, before walking off, cursing loudly. When you feel the coast is clear, you come out from behind cover and open the leather shoulder bag to find 1 Gold Piece, a small box of fish hooks, and a small bag of salt. You take the items you want, and also the bow and six arrows fired at you, which are lying nearby. You fill your flask from the stream and take a long drink of cool water. Add 1 *STAMINA* point. Turn to **345**.

56

You reach an area of tall grass which is waist-height in parts, and draw your sword in case some unseen enemy might pounce on you. Something momentarily blocks out the sun overhead, and you look up to see a gigantic predatory bird flying west. With its huge wingspan, curved black beak and fire-red feathers, there's no mistaking the WARHAWK. A large wicker basket is gripped in its talons, and appears to contain a huge block of stone. Suddenly the Warhawk lets go of the basket with one foot, and it swings down, forcing the giant bird to bank sharply to the right, losing height. It is unable to recover and lets go of the basket completely. It soars back up into the sky and flies off, squawking loudly. The basket plummets to the ground, and you hear loud screams coming from inside the basket, which lands in the tall grass with a dull thud, disappearing from view. The screams are replaced by groans coming from where the basket landed. If you want to investigate, turn to **72**. If you would rather keep walking towards Darkwood Forest, turn to **114**.

57

The necklace is cursed and will bring you bad luck and make you weak. Reduce your *LUCK* and *SKILL* scores by 2 points. Not yet aware of the effects of the cursed necklace, you walk over to the iron chest. Turn to **212**.

58

There are three streets by which you could leave the market square. Will you:

Head west down Silver Street?	Turn to **104**
Head north down Armoury Lane?	Turn to **8**
Head east down Beggar's Alley?	Turn to **283**

59

You amble across Palace Square and pick up a loose cobblestone without anybody noticing. You creep up behind the guard, hitting him on the back of his head with the large stone. He falls backwards and you catch him in your arms, dragging him down Palace Street into Snake Alley. You put on the guard's black chain-mail vest, studded shoulder pads, black cloak and iron helmet, which virtually covers your face. As you pick up his sword and shield, you realize you are being watched by a gang of thieves who followed you into the alleyway. 'You better leave something for us or else!' their burly, scar-faced leader says threateningly. You tell him they can keep anything they want, pushing past him to walk into the street to go back to Palace Square to wait for the changing of the guard. You don't have to wait long before ten guards march out of the palace grounds to relieve the ones on duty outside. You join the guards returning to the palace, marching along at the back of the line into the palace grounds, passing Stinkfoot and Twoteeth at the gates. Turn to **86**.

60

The three arrows aimed at you clatter into your shield, and ricochet off it to land harmlessly on the ground. You reach the bandits before they have time to reload, swinging your sword through the air. Fight them one at a time.

	SKILL	STAMINA
First BANDIT	6	7
Second BANDIT	7	7
Third BANDIT	7	6

If you win, turn to **22**.

61

You are breathing heavily after the fight with the Hippohog, and go back to sleep immediately. You do not receive any other unwelcome visitors and wake up not long after dawn. You gather up your belongings and begin your climb of Moonstone Hills, determined to reach Skull Crag by noon. Turn to **368**.

62

There is so much red dust in the air that you cannot help but breathe some of it in. The spores floating inside the dust cloud are toxic and you begin to cough violently. You drop to your knees, clutching your throat, with your lungs feeling like they are on fire. There is nothing you can do to stop yourself from suffocating. The Sporeball has found a new host for its spores to grow into fungal parasites. Your adventure is over.

63

You hurry down Harbour Street past a row of fishermen's cottages on the right-hand side. The left-hand side of the street is lined with small supply shops catering mainly to seafarers. There is a sign above one of the small shop windows which says Finbar's Fireworks. The wooden entrance door is slightly ajar. If you want to go in the shop, turn to **300**. If you want to keep walking towards Singing Bridge, turn to **118**.

64

You walk out of the main gates of Chalice heading north, looking back briefly at the town's rooftops and towers sticking out above the outer wall. You follow a well-worn path past a church ruin and ancient graveyard, and on, past scattered dwellings until you reach a farm where the path ends at the edge of a vast field of golden corn, the tall stems swaying slowly from side to side in the gentle breeze. It's going to be a bumper crop, and good news for the farmers whose oxen will soon be hauling wooden carts through the field for their farmhands to load with cobs of corn. Looking north as far as you can see, way beyond the cornfield, you can just make out the top of a high wall of trees that marks the edge of Darkwood Forest, the vast forest that is home to the grand, and sometimes grumpy, old wizard Yaztromo, who lives alone in his fabled tower. Many a tale and myth have come from Darkwood Forest, but you remind yourself that Skull Crag is your destination today. You look at your map and head east in the warm sunlight, eager to reach Moonstone Hills before nightfall. As you walk along the edge of the cornfield lost in thought, you suddenly hear the sound of galloping hooves and the shrill call of a hunting horn. If you want to face the rider coming towards you, turn to **263**. If you would rather hide in the cornfield, turn to **148**.

65

You wait until the bandits are in full view before firing arrows rapidly at them. Roll one die. The number rolled is the number of bandits who receive fatal wounds from your arrows. If you killed all six bandits, turn to **372**. If you killed five bandits, turn to **350**. If you killed less than five bandits, **302**.

Stormheart gallops on, his dark mane swishing across his neck and his tail streaming behind in the wind. Onwards you ride with the noise of his thundering hooves loud in your ear. Silver River comes into view on your left, and ahead you see where it joins Catfish River. To your right you see a narrow wooden bridge which spans the river. You slow down to a trot and steer Stormheart over to the bridge. There is nobody about. There is a wooden coin box fixed to the handrail which is carved with runes. There is a rhyme written on a wooden sign above the box which reads, *Pay 1 Gold Piece, and cross in peace. Pay nothing at all, and be sure to fall.* It is signed *Bartholomew Black*. If you want to put 1 Gold Piece into the box to cross Black's Bridge, turn to **32**. If you want to cross the river without paying, turn to **374**.

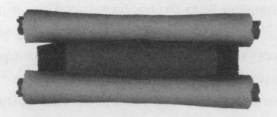

67

The zombie corpse twitches on the cellar floor before finally coming to rest. Your eyes adjust to the gloom and you see that the cellar has bare stone walls and is no more than six square metres in size. The words *help me* are written in dried blood on one of the walls. There is also an arrow drawn in blood on the opposite wall which points to a small crack in the wall. Suddenly you hear footsteps from above. Somebody has entered the cottage and is walking across the floorboards towards the trapdoor. If you want to run up the steps to confront the unknown visitor, turn to **352**. If you would rather stay where you are, turn to **109**.

68

You climb on board the cart and talk to the ruddy-faced driver, who tells you that he is a farmer taking a delivery of corn and carrots to Largo, a small village on the banks of Catfish River west of Darkwood Forest. You scan the horizon, looking for the elusive Chaos Warrior, but don't see anybody who looks remotely like him. You keep thinking about Hakasan, who you have left injured and alone in Darkwood Forest, and hope she is safe. You arrive in Largo in the afternoon, and thank the farmer for the ride. The villagers are friendly river folk, who spend their days ferrying people and goods up and down Catfish River on their flat-bottomed boats. You walk round Largo asking everybody you meet if they have seen a Chaos Warrior in the vicinity. The replies are all negative until you talk to one very tall and stocky man by the name of Onx, who tells you that his cousin was paid 5 Gold Pieces to take a Chaos Warrior to Port Blacksand earlier in the day. 'My cousin was too frightened to say no. I can ferry you to Port Blacksand for 2 Gold Pieces if you wish?' the boatman says in a friendly voice. If you want to accept his offer, turn to **303**. If you would rather refuse his offer and head back to help Hakasan, turn to **9**.

You watch the creature uncurl and flip over on to four spindly crab-like legs

69

You reach a section of the tunnel where the floor is littered with rocks and rubble. One of the rocks appears to move, and you realize that it is not a rock but a grey-coloured creature. It is no bigger than a cannonball, and its plated exoskeleton looks to be almost as hard. You watch the creature uncurl and flip over on to four spindly, crab-like legs. Its small head has large compound black eyes, long antennae, and mouthparts with three rows of sharp mandibles which it uses to inject venom into its victims to paralyse them and feed off their blood. Two more GRONKS flip over and scuttle towards you. Fight them one at a time.

	SKILL	STAMINA
First GRONK	5	5
Second GRONK	5	4
Third GRONK	5	4

If you win the battle without losing any Attack Rounds, turn to **208**. If you win but lose one or more Attack Rounds, turn to **354**.

70

You place an arrow in the bowstring, drawing it back until it is fully loaded. You know you only have time for one shot, which needs to pierce the Demon's eye socket to have any effect. With Hakasan screaming at you to fire, you take careful aim and release the arrow. You watch it fly towards its mark, but it misses Zanbar Bone's skull by inches. If you own a Demon Dagger, turn to **45**. If you do not have the dagger, you will have to fight on with your sword. Turn to **138**.

71

The building is a small wood cabin in front of which there are many rows of blueberry bushes blooming with plump, ripe fruit. There is a scarecrow wearing a straw hat tied to a wooden post in the middle of the rows of bushes which seems to be keeping the birds at bay. If you want to take a closer look, turn to **358**. If you would rather continue your journey east to Moonstone Hills, turn to **134**.

72

You stride through the tall grass as fast as you can in the direction of the groaning man. *Test Your Luck*. If you are Lucky, turn to **24**. If you are Unlucky, turn to **217**.

73

You give Onx 2 Gold Pieces in payment for the dice, which he says are made of animal bone. You notice that the number 1 on the dice has been replaced by a clover leaf. He tells you that you have bought a pair of 'Lucky Bones'. Add 2 *LUCK* points. You bid farewell to Onx and leave Largo to head back to Darkwood Forest, walking as quickly as possible. A few hours later, you are back at the spot where you left Hakasan in the forest, but are alarmed to discover that she is not there. You wonder if maybe you are in the wrong place, but are certain the tree you are standing next to is the same one Hakasan was leaning against when you left her. 'You took your time, didn't you?' a familiar voice calls out from above. You look up to see Hakasan staring down at you from a branch of the tree. You ask her how she managed to climb the tree with a broken ankle, to which she replies, 'I used a rope to help pull myself up. It's safer up here! Well, did you deal with Klash?' You reply that you failed to find him, unfortunately, and explain what happened. She lowers herself down to the ground, sits down, and says, 'That's not good, but we can't give up now.' You see that her ankle is very swollen and tell her that you hope you will be able to fix it up, handing her the bottle given to you by Onx. She asks what it is, and you reply that it was sold to you as healing potion. 'After you, then!' Hakasan says, smiling. If you want to drink some of the liquid first, turn to **351**. If you want to insist that Hakasan drinks it, turn to **122**.

74

You decide to give 1 Copper Piece to each of the three beggars closest to you. They all nod in recognition of your generosity. The oldest of the three begins to speak in a low but calm voice. 'Thank you, stranger. You are most kind, especially since I see from your appearance that your luck is not much better than ours. How times change. My friend here was once a fine jewellery maker until he lost his right arm fighting off robbers in Port Blacksand. If there is anything we could do for you in return for your kindness, please say.' If you want to ask the one-armed man if he's heard of Gurnard Jaggle, turn to **378**. If you would rather bid them farewell and walk on to the T-junction at the end of the alley, turn to **311**.

75

The bearded man shouts 'Yes!', punching the air in triumph. He holds his hand out to await his prize, which you take from your backpack to give him. He holds the ruby up to the light, inspecting it closely to make sure it is genuine. Satisfied it is a *genuine* gemstone, he shakes your hand, and you head back to the bar, feeling annoyed that you lost your valuable ruby. Turn to **89**.

76

After picking up her sword, Hakasan puts your arm around her neck and half carries and half drags you towards the cover of a fallen tree. Before you get there, another flight of arrows whistles through the air. *Test Your Luck*. If you are Lucky, turn to **312**. If you are Unlucky, turn to **220**.

77

You just have enough time to reload the flintlock and fire again, but without taking careful aim. Roll two dice and add 2 to the total. If the number is equal to or less than your *SKILL* score, turn to **267**. If the number is greater than your *SKILL* score, the lead ball misses Zanbar Bone. There is no time to reload, and you draw your sword in one last desperate attempt to defeat the Demon. Turn to **138**.

78

As soon as you have finished your breakfast, Yaztromo hands you 15 Gold Pieces and tells you to get ready to depart. You meet him on the ground floor, where he asks you to touch the tips of the fingers of your non-fighting arm with the fingertips of his opposite hand. A bolt of energy suddenly shoots up your arm and you immediately feel incredibly fit and healthy. Increase your *STAMINA* score by 10 points. Turn to **272**.

79

You light your lantern and walk in slowly to find yourself in a large cave which has charcoal drawings of gruesome beasts covering the walls. The cave is empty but you notice the tunnel entrance at the back, which is quite narrow and less than two metres high. The air inside the tunnel is cool and still, and has a slight musty smell. You walk down it to where it ends at a junction. If you want to go left, turn to **370**. If you want to go right, turn to **203**.

80

You cross the market square and walk down Thread Street. In your hurry to find Nicodemus, you are less mindful of danger than usual, and do not notice a gang of masked men armed with clubs slip out of Snake Alley and creep up on you from behind. *Test Your Luck*. If you are Lucky, turn to **261**. If you are Unlucky, turn to **290**.

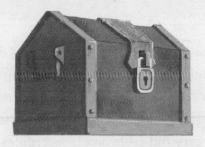

81

'Excellent. Let's go!' Hakasan says enthusiastically. You exit the cave together, stepping outside on to the ledge where the bright sunlight hurts your eyes, making you squint. You scramble down the crag to the main entrance to the cave. Peering inside, you see nothing but dark shadows beyond the sunlit entrance. 'I wouldn't go in there if I were you,' the ninja tracker warns. 'Let's head west to the Eastern Plain.' You walk back down the valley, exchanging stories about your adventures, when suddenly two tall, ugly creatures with tusked mouths and long hair braided with bones jump out from behind a large rock. They are wearing animal furs, and advance towards you swinging their spiked clubs above their heads. They are HILL TROLLS and you must fight them. You opt to take on the taller of the two.

HILL TROLL   *SKILL 9*   *STAMINA 9*

If you win, turn to **102**.

82

Silver Street ends at a T-junction where it joins a narrow cobbled street running north and south. It is lined with drab, narrow houses built of grey stone with small windows and high-pitched roofs. A horse-driven cart laden with rusty old iron, worn-out shoes and clothes, rotten wood and bits of old furniture rumbles down the street towards you. The pasty-faced driver is slouched in his seat in a threadbare coat and top hat looking bored, occasionally flicking his horse with a long whip to urge it on. 'Rag and bone!' he shouts out half-heartedly as he passes each house, hoping that somebody might toss something out for him to take away. But nobody opens their door. There doesn't appear to be much happening in Barrel Street. Will you:

Stop the rag-and-bone man to talk to him?   Turn to **326**

Walk back to the market square
to go to Armoury Lane?   Turn to **8**

Walk back to the market square
to go to Beggar's Alley?   Turn to **283**

83

The arrow whistles past your head and thuds harmlessly into a tree behind you. Turn to **372**.

84

The vegetable soup tastes good. Add 2 *STAMINA* points. If you have not done so already, you can either take a look at the books (turn to **331**) or open the wooden chest (turn to **376**). If you would rather leave the tree house and carry on towards Yaztromo's Tower, turn to **251**.

85

As soon as you slip the bracelet on to your wrist, a strange tingling feeling runs through your body which makes your limbs feel numb and heavy. It's a huge effort even to lift your arm or walk one step. The tingling sensation quickly subsides, leaving you feeling stronger than ever and full of energy. Gain 1 *SKILL* point and 2 *STAMINA* points. Pleased to be wearing the Bracelet of Power, you leave the cottage and set off again for Moonstone Hills. Turn to **164**.

The palace grounds are a vast area of gardens, trees and courtyards divided by a sweeping carriageway leading to the coach house, stables, servants' quarters and barracks for the household guards. A paved path leads from the carriageway up to a wide stone staircase to the imposing main doors of the house. Windowless at ground level, the house looks fortress-like and impossible to enter. You follow the guards to the barracks, where they take off their helmets and armour and sit down to relax. You do likewise, and start talking to the guard sitting next to you. You tell him that you are a new conscript, and are interested to know where prisoners should be taken after they have been arrested. 'Nobody is allowed to enter the house, so don't use the main door or you'll end up in the cells yourself,' the guard warns. 'There is a maze of dungeon corridors under the main building where the cells and a torture chamber are located. You'll find the entrance door to the cells on the north side of the palace.' You thank him for the information and stand up to help yourself to a mug of water left out for the guards. Add 1 *STAMINA* point. You put your helmet back on and, when nobody is watching, walk behind the barracks and on past the servants' quarters down a gravel path which leads to the north side of the house where there are stone steps leading down to a narrow entranceway. There is nobody about and you hurry down the steps to an iron door which is locked. If you own a bunch of brass keys, turn to **230**. If you don't have any brass keys, you have no choice but to knock on the door. Turn to **125**.

87

Immersed in thought, you are not as alert as you should be in the forest, and step unwittingly into the hidden jaws of a cast-iron animal trap which snaps shut on your ankle. Try as you might, you are unable to open it. The hours pass, and twice during the morning wolves come sniffing, and you have to fend them off with your sword. Animal trappers finally arrive, but unfortunately they are Man-Orcs. Instead of rescuing you, they tie you to a tree, and take all the items from your backpack. Deduct these items from your Adventure Sheet. You struggle to free yourself, worried that the wolves might return at any moment, but the knots are tied too tightly. Suddenly you hear the noise of a twig breaking underfoot. Fearing the worst, you get ready to kick out at the oncoming predator. 'Need some help?' you hear a familiar voice ask. Standing in front of you is Hakasan with a big grin on her face. Suddenly her expression changes, and she says in a serious voice, 'We can't just ignore what happened back there. I couldn't walk away without knowing the truth. But I'm only going to free you if agree to come with me to find Yaztromo. We have to warn him. He might be under attack even as we speak.' You agree that her reasoning makes perfect sense, and apologize for thinking otherwise earlier. She cuts the rope binding you to the tree, and you pick up your empty backpack, left behind by the Man-Orcs. They also left your water bottle on the ground, and your sword, which they threw into the undergrowth, preferring spiked clubs as their weapon of choice. 'Deep down I knew you would come with me. Come on, let's go,' Hakasan says with a wry smile. Turn to **252**.

The old man who was robbed by the girl pushes his way to the front of the circle of angry people. 'Nobody robbed this girl,' he says angrily, pointing at her. 'I was the person who was robbed – most likely by her! Search her!' The girl kicks out, trying to keep the crowd at bay, but fails to do so. She is forced to hand the leather pouch back to the old man. A large, bearded man with braces holding up his baggy britches silences the crowd and says in a commanding voice, 'Put her in the stocks for the rest of the morning. Let it be a lesson to her and a warning to others. Have your rotten tomatoes at the ready!' The old man turns to you, smiles, and shakes your hand in gratitude. 'Thank you, stranger,' he says warmly. 'The money in the pouch is payment for a month's work! I just collected it from a customer. That thieving girl must have followed me here from Lion Street.' If you want to ask the old man what he does for a living, turn to **298**. If you want to bid farewell to him, turn to **26**.

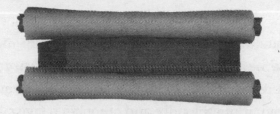

89

Whilst walking back to the bar, a brightly dressed woman with rosy cheeks and fluttering eyelashes squeezes through the crowd and bumps into you, apologizing profusely. You are momentarily distracted, and do not notice her accomplice slip his hand inside your backpack to help himself to your belongings. Roll one die twice to determine which items are stolen from your backpack:

Die Roll	Item Stolen
1 ⟶	2 Gold Pieces
2 ⟶	3 Gold Pieces
3 ⟶	All keys
4 ⟶	Brass bell and 1 Gold Piece
5 ⟶	Knife and 1 Gold Piece
6 ⟶	A bottle of potion

You reach the bar without knowing that you have been pickpocketed. If you have not done so already, you may talk to the innkeeper (turn to **317**). If you would rather leave the tavern and head down Harbour Street towards Singing Bridge, turn to **63**.

90

'Nobody enters my lair and makes demands of me,' the Norgul says angrily. It is a powerful creature which fights with brute strength and savage aggression. Enraged, it roars loudly and launches a frenzied attack on you with flailing fists, eager to feast on your eyes. Its thick hide is not easy to pierce, even with your sharp-edged sword.

NORGUL   SKILL 10   STAMINA 9

If you win, turn to **231**.

91

You stand in front of the advancing horse and cart with your hands raised in the air. The driver pulls hard on his reins, shouting 'Whoa!' at the top of his voice to bring his horse to a halt. You ask him if he has seen any sign of a Chaos Warrior in the last few hours. He shakes his head and says, 'I personally haven't seen one of those ruthless mercenaries, but a trapper who was out catching rabbits in the fields earlier today told me that he'd seen a Chaos Warrior come out of the forest and head west towards Catfish River. The trapper didn't go near him, and ran most of the way back to Chalice fearing for his life. I'm headed towards Catfish River myself. I'll give you a lift for 1 Gold Piece if you are agreeable?' If you want to pay for a ride, turn to **68**. If you would rather decline his offer, turn to **260**.

92

You lift the lid off the barrel, releasing two very large RATS which were trapped inside. They leap out, one of them jumping on to your shoulder. Gripping your tunic with its sharp claws, it leaps forward to bite your neck. Roll two dice. If the number rolled is equal to or less than your *SKILL* score, turn to **48**. If the number rolled is greater than your *SKILL* score, turn to **147**.

'I'm Travis Traynor the travelling trader!'

93

The man puts his sack down on the ground and sits down with a sigh on his tripod stool, introducing himself by saying, 'Good morning. I'm Travis Traynor, the travelling trader! Would you be so kind as to look at my wares?' Without waiting for an answer, he empties the contents of the sack on to the ground. There is a lot of junk on the ground, but three things catch your eye – an onyx orb, a sword made of dazzling steel and a copper hunting horn. 'You've got an eye for fine things, my friend,' says Travis. 'Allow me to tell you the price of these priceless items! The Orb of Obedience is on sale for 10 Gold Pieces. I'm asking 10 Gold Pieces for the Horn of Calling, and the Venom Sword will cost you 20 Gold Pieces, which, might I say, is a bargain. You won't find a sharper sword in Allansia. It's sharper than a One-Eye, and it is charged with magic energy that's so powerful it can even defeat the Demon Spawn of the Netherworld.' You buy the items you can afford, paying Travis before getting back into the saddle to ride to Darkwood Forest. Turn to **286**.

94

The vial shatters on impact with the rocky ground, and a cloud of green gas escapes from the broken glass. The gas spirals towards you, enveloping you and making you choke. You run away, gasping for air, but cannot escape the poisonous gas cloud. You drop to your knees, clutching your throat, and fall unconscious. Your adventure is over.

95

As you bend down to fill your flask, you suddenly hear the sound of rocks tumbling down from above. You spin round to see a huge boulder rolling down the side of the steep hill towards you, and dive sideways to try to avoid being crushed by it. Roll two dice. If the number rolled is less than or equal to your *SKILL* score, turn to **394**. If the number rolled is greater than your *SKILL* score, turn to **182**.

96

You are in such a deep sleep that you are unaware of the huge SCORPION BUG which emerges from its nearby borehole. Virtually blind, Scorpion Bugs detect even the slightest vibrations on the surface aboveground. It is attracted by your breathing, and crawls out of its hole to inject you with the paralysis-inducing sting at the end of its plated exoskeleton body. It ensnares you with its sharp pincer-like claws and drags you down into its borehole, where it will feed on you in the coming weeks. Your adventure is over.

97

You hear the sound of footsteps approaching from the other side of the door, followed by a bolt sliding in its metal bracket. The door is opened by an enormous bald-headed man, who is wearing a tight-fitting black jacket with tails over a white shirt tucked into black, knee-length britches, with long red socks and shiny black shoes completing the butler's attire. His eyes are narrow and slightly slanted, and he looks at you with suspicion. 'Yes?' he asks tersely. If you want to say that you have come to collect a letter, turn to **53**. If you want to say that you are an adventurer down on your luck who is looking for work as a guard, turn to **44**.

98

The light quickly fades as the sun sinks below the horizon, but the moon shines brightly in the clear night sky, casting an eerie twilight across the landscape. Suddenly you hear a familiar voice calling out to you. 'Good to see you have got a fire burning.' *Test Your Luck*. If you are Lucky, turn to **324**. If you are Unlucky, turn to **185**.

99

'Well, I've been wandering around this forest for quite some time now, and I've yet to find any gold. It certainly doesn't grow on trees!' Bignose says, chortling loudly. 'If I were you, I'd try your luck in Firetop Mountain. They say the place is filled with gold. Or there's always Baron Sukhumvit's Deathtrap Dungeon in Fang. Lots of gold to be won there if you manage to come out alive. Nobody ever has mind you. Right, I must be on my way. I've got my second cousin to find. Cheerio!' The Dwarf walks past you, whistling happily to himself, and is soon out of sight. Turn to **246**.

100

You pick yourself up out of the dirt, none the worse for wear, and watch the horseman disappear west in a cloud of dust. Whoever it was on horseback is certainly in a hurry. You decide you might as well help yourself to some corn. Add 1 *STAMINA* point. Looking east, you estimate it will be dark by the time you reach Skull Crag and hope you will be able to find somewhere safe to camp down for the night. Looking south, you see a semi-ruined stone cottage with its thatched roof mostly missing because of a fire. If you want to take a look inside the cottage, turn to **319**. If you would rather press on towards Moonstone Hills, turn to **164**.

101

Roll two dice, and add 4 to the total if you are using Lucky Bones. If the number is 8 or higher, turn to **366**. If the total is 7 or less, turn to **75**.

102

You look round to see Hakasan wiping Trolls' blood off the razor-sharp blade of her magnificent sword. 'They never learn, stupid creatures,' she says dismissively. A search of the Trolls' pouches yields 3 Gold Pieces and two silver buttons. 'Well, it's a start!' she says cheerfully. You set off again, talking about past adventures, with Hakasan asking lots of questions. 'You never did tell me what you found in Skull Crag, only that the treasure was missing from the iron chest.' You reply saying you found a wooden box in the iron chest which you take out of your backpack to show her. She takes it from you, and on seeing the carved beetle motif on the lid, says, 'This looks like one of Gurnard Jaggle's deadly puzzle boxes. You have to be very careful when opening these.' She turns it over and over, examining it carefully. She presses down on the lid and, at the same time, pushes her thumb against one side of the box. A small section of wood slides out. She repeats the action on the other sides of the box until there are four sections of wood sticking out. With a look of intense concentration on her face, she carefully lifts the lid, breathing a sigh of relief when it's open, and says, 'Phew! Now what have we got here?'

A white-haired old man ... is placing jewellery and ornaments in the window

There are three items in the puzzle box: a small glass vial with green gas swirling around inside, a small lead ball and a folded piece of paper. 'Gurnard didn't disappoint us. The green gas is most likely poisonous. What are you going to do with the vial?' she asks, inspecting it closely before handing it to you. If you want to put the vial in your backpack, turn to **321**. If you want to throw it as far away as possible, turn to **150**.

103

You dab a small amount of paste on to your wound. It immediately stops hurting and visibly starts to heal. In less than five minutes there is no sign of the wound, not even the slightest scar. Add 1 *STAMINA* point and 1 *LUCK* point. You put the cork back in the jar and pack it away with the bandage before leaving the tree house to go back to Hakasan. Turn to **325**.

104

Silver Street is a narrow cobbled street lined with small houses and shops, most of which are jeweller's and silversmith's. There are beautifully crafted silver teapots, urns, platters and condiment sets on display in the window of the silversmith's. The second shop has a sign above the shop window which says *Jethro's Jewels*. A white-haired old man wearing a white shirt and a black apron is placing gold jewellery and ornaments in the window. He looks up, smiles, and beckons you to enter his shop, hoping that you might be his first customer of the day. You pop your head through the door and see a tall Man-Orc standing near the jeweller, who is his hired guard. If you want to enter the jeweller's shop, turn to **275**. If you would rather keep on walking to the end of the street, turn to **82**.

105

The burning-hot fireroot juice does the job, triggering the holes covering the Sporeball to close up, and preventing any further spores from being released into the air. *Test Your Luck*. If you are Lucky, turn to **131**. If you are Unlucky, turn to **62**.

106

Your rowing boat is met by hail of crossbow bolts, one of them sinking into your thigh. Lose 2 *STAMINA* points. You ignore the pain, and pull on the oars with gritted teeth. Nicodemus mutters more arcane words, creating an invisible shield which is only evident when you see crossbow bolts deflecting off it to land harmlessly in the river. You pass under the arch of the city wall, rowing away from Port Blacksand as fast as you can. There is no time to stop, and Luannah has to pull the bolt from your leg whilst you continue to row, binding the bleeding wound as best she can. Finally assured that nobody is in pursuit, you settle down to row at a gentler pace upriver, and discuss the threat of Zanbar Bone with Nicodemus. Turn to **379**.

You crawl inside your bivouac, roll out your blanket and lie down exhausted after a hard day's walk. A full moon rises in the night sky and you stare at the bright stars, thinking about the events of the day before drifting off to sleep. You have not been asleep for long when you are woken by some snuffling sounds. You sit up, grab your sword and peer outside. Suddenly you see something moving in the pale moonlight. It's a large, round black shape, and it is headed towards you on four stumpy legs, its snuffling sounds getting louder and louder. A cloud that was partially blocking out the moon drifts away and you see the creature standing in front of you. It has a huge head with an enormous tusked mouth, wide snout, tiny eyes and ears, and a thick-set neck that joins its head to its bulbous body covered with a thick grey hide. Its keen sense of smell has led the HIPPOHOG to you, looking for its evening meal. On seeing you, the Hippohog breaks wind, releasing a stench that is so rancid that it makes you retch and feel light-headed. Hippohogs overcome their prey by first disabling them with their acrid intestinal gas before trampling them underfoot. You feel quite sick, but know you have to drag yourself outside to fight the Hippohog. You barely feel able to lift your sword. Reduce your *SKILL* by 3 points for this battle.

HIPPOHOG	*SKILL* 9	*STAMINA* 8

If you win, turn to **61**.

Gurnard Jaggle walks across the room and sits down on the edge of his bed. 'As you may have heard, I like gold, but gold doesn't like me. It seems to avoid me at all costs. So I thank you for these 3 Gold Pieces. You may know that I am a failed treasure hunter. For years I tried to find gold, but only did once. But I was robbed of it, and became very angry, and decided to take my anger out on other treasure hunters. I began making booby-trapped wooden puzzle boxes, making them very hard to open. I put a vial of poisonous gas inside the boxes, like the one I am holding now, and left them in caves and dungeons, hoping a treasure hunter would find them and smash them open to release the gas. I have regretted it ever since. I hope nobody actually died from trying to open one of my boxes.' Hakasan tells Gurnard that unfortunately he may have caused one or two fatalities. With tears in his eyes, Gurnard apologizes over and over again, and asks how he might atone for his crimes. You tell him that you believe Allansia will be in grave danger when Zanbar Bone returns from his twilight existence, and that is why you are on your way to warn Yaztromo about an imminent attack on his tower. You tell Gurnard that anything he could do to help would go a long way to absolve him. Gurnard looks at you, trembling. 'The only person who knows how to defeat Zanbar Bone is the wizard Nicodemus. I found the iron chest in the Crystal Cave but there wasn't any gold inside. Somebody else got there before me. But they missed the greatest treasure of all – the Ring of Burning Snakes, the fabled ring that once belonged to Nicodemus. I found it on the floor near the empty chest. It must have fallen out when the treasure hunters opened the chest in their hurry to take the golden amulets. But alas, I no longer have the ring. It was taken from me by a Chaos Warrior by the name of Klash. He ambushed me when I came home last night. There was nothing I could do to stop him taking the ring. I'm lucky to still be alive. I fear Klash has been hired by Bone's most faithful servant, Lord Azzur. Somehow he must have known that I had the ring. I'm certain the ring has special powers which Nicodemus could use to defeat Zanbar Bone.' Hakasan looks at you anxiously and says, 'What do we do now? Should we track down the Chaos Warrior or warn Yaztromo first?' If you want to chase after Klash, turn to **43**. If you would rather leave immediately and press on to Yaztromo's Tower, turn to **251**.

109

An ugly green face appears at the top of the stairs and glares down at you. It's another MAN-ORC and it is very angry to find its friends lying dead on the floor. It points at you and starts screaming and shouting in a language you don't understand. Before you have time to do anything, the Man-Orc slams the trapdoor down and bolts it shut. You hear something being dragged across the floorboards and realize the Man-Orc is sliding the iron stove on top of the trapdoor to make sure you don't escape. You hear footsteps walking away and the front door being closed. You are left alone in pitch-black darkness, and there is no way out. Your adventure is over.

You tell Onx that you have to go, and bid him farewell. You leave Largo to head in the direction of Darkwood Forest, walking as quickly as possible. A few hours later, you are back at the spot where you left Hakasan in the forest, but are alarmed to discover that she is not there. You wonder if maybe you are in the wrong place, but are certain the tree you are standing next to is the same one Hakasan was leaning against when you left her. 'You took your time, didn't you?' a familiar voice calls out from above. You look up to see Hakasan staring down at you from a branch of the tree. You ask her how she managed to climb the tree with a broken ankle, to which she replies, 'I used a rope to help pull myself up. It's safer up here! Well, did you deal with Klash?' You reply that you failed to find him and explain what happened. She lowers herself down to the ground, sits down, and says, 'That's not good, but we can't give up now.' You see that her ankle is very swollen and tell her that you hope you will be able to fix it up, handing her the bottle given to you by Onx. She asks what it is, and you reply that it was sold to you as a healing potion. 'After you, then!' Hakasan says, smiling. If you want to drink some of the liquid first, turn to **351**. If you want to insist that Hakasan drinks it, turn to **122**.

111

Ahead you see the tunnel opens up again and find yourself in an enormous underground limestone cave. Huge crystal stalactites hang down from the high ceiling which sparkles in the light from your lantern. Water drips down from the tips of long and short stalactites into pools on the cave floor, echoing loudly. You are excited to think you might be standing in the Crystal Cave shown on Murgat Shurr's map. You notice that the ceiling to your right has a large round hole in it, as though something had bored its way through, and there is a patch of transparent goo on the floor directly underneath the hole. At the back of the cave there is a large shard of crystal lying on the cave floor with an iron chest placed on it. If you want to walk over to look inside the chest, turn to **289**. If you would rather take a closer look at the hole in the ceiling, turn to **399**.

112

You put a Gold Piece in the mug and tentatively lower yourself on to the wooden throne. You think carefully about the wish you want to make when suddenly the mug is pulled up on the string and disappears into the leaves. You hear high-pitched giggling high up in the tree and realize that you have been cheated out of your money. Lose 1 *LUCK*

point. You look up but don't see anybody. 'That giggling sounds like CHUMPIES to me,' Hakasan says, shaking her head. 'They are always coming up with new ways to steal gold from people. They love gold. If we could only get our hands on those mischievous little thieves, we'd be rich! We might as well keep going as we'll never catch them.' Annoyed at yourself for falling for the Chumpies' trick, you walk on, cursing. Turn to **348**.

113

The ugly Ogre is a powerful and very vicious opponent. It is skilled at using a wooden club as a weapon, and swings it forcefully through the air.

OGRE   *SKILL 8*   *STAMINA 10*

If you win, turn to **179**.

114

You walk on, and suddenly feel something warm and wet land on your head with a splat. You look up to see the Warhawk circling overhead and understand the grim reality of what has landed on you. Lose 1 *LUCK* point. The soggy poop starts to trickle down the side of your head and has a very unpleasant smell. You wash it off with water from your flask, but the smell lingers. 'That will teach you not to ignore a cry for help!' Hakasan says, trying not to laugh. You curse your luck and decide to head back in the direction of where the basket landed. Turn to **72**.

115

You swing your sword down as hard as you can on the bloated creeper which erupts under the blow. Purple sap squirts out everywhere, fizzing on contact with everything it touches. *Test Your Luck*. If you are Lucky, turn to **49**. If you are Unlucky, turn to **243**.

116

As soon as you run off, the little old man screams, 'Don't leave me, friend! Don't leave me!' With his words ringing in your ears, you run through the tall grasses as fast as you can, and soon leave the short-legged Blue Imps behind. When they are out of sight, you slow down to a walk, heading in the direction of Moonstone Hills. Turn to **134**.

117

You see an old tree trunk with crumbling, rotten bark which is host to a cluster of fiery-red capped mushrooms. Your stomach rumbles noisily and you realize just how hungry you are after your exploits in Skull Crag. Hakasan sees you looking at the mushrooms and shouts at you not to eat them, as they might be poisonous. If you want to eat the mushrooms, turn to **285**. If you would rather heed her advice and go back to help her look for tracks, turn to **304**.

A fearsome-looking giant of a man

After passing Parrot Lane and Garden Street on your left, you turn right between two small gatehouses on to Singing Bridge. It is a narrow, rickety wooden bridge with a gruesome collection of skulls skewered on wooden spikes fixed to the handrail. The wind sounds like tortured souls wailing as it blows through the skulls. Whilst crossing the bridge, you witness a kidnapping. A white-haired old man with a long beard and wearing white robes is being dragged in chains up a small flight of wooden steps from underneath the bridge by two tall guards wearing black chain-mail vests and iron helmets. The old man is not struggling, and appears to be semi-conscious. You realize it is Nicodemus, the legendary Grand Wizard of Allansia. Directing the guards is a fearsome-looking giant of a man wearing plate metal armour under a crimson tunic through which iron spikes protrude from his shoulder plates. He is wearing a horned helmet which is etched with demonic symbols, and carrying a heavy two-handed sword. There is no mistaking the CHAOS WARRIOR, and you know it must be Klash who is in charge of the kidnapping. Without thinking about the consequences, you run forward to attack Klash with your sword.

CHAOS WARRIOR   SKILL 10   STAMINA 11

If you win, turn to **313**.

119

As the smoke clears away, you are distraught to see that Zanbar Bone is still standing. You missed! The Demon Prince vents his fury, foaming at the mouth with anger, and calls on his troops to press forward. If you possess another lead ball and want to shoot at him again, turn to **77**. If you do not have another lead ball, you can either attack Zanbar Bone with your sword (turn to **138**) or, if you own a Demon Dagger, you could throw it at his head (turn to **356**).

120

Bignose pauses to look at his treasured weapon for a second before saying, 'Done! I'm not going to argue with anybody who is going to help Yaztromo. The battleaxe is yours!' You thank Bignose for his generosity, and give him the goblet and bell in exchange. He smiles, saying, 'Right, I must be on my way. I've got my second cousin to find. Cheerio!' The Dwarf walks past you, whistling happily to himself, and is soon out of sight. Turn to **246**.

121

The stricken vampire bug twitches spasmodically on the ground before coming to rest. Though their larvae start life in dormant pools of water, vampire bugs are not usually found in towns, preferring to suck the blood of injured animals in the wild. A young urchin runs up to you and suggests that you rub the vampire bug's blood on your skin as it will give you strength. He asks for a Copper Piece for the advice. If you want to do this, turn to **166**. If you would rather walk on to the T-junction, turn to **206**.

122

You hand the bottle to Hakasan, telling her not to worry. She snatches it from you, scowls and gulps down the potion. Her scowl soon turns to a smile, and she says with glee that her ankle feels suddenly strong and free from pain. Minutes later the swelling is gone, and she is able to stand and put her full weight on the ankle. 'That's incredible! Thank you, thank you, thank you,' she says happily. She hands the bottle back to you, and you drink the last drops left in it. Add 1 *STAMINA* point. You suggest that you should stick with the original plan and go to Yaztromo's Tower to warn him about Zanbar Bone. You take the lead, hacking your way through bushes and thick undergrowth of dense part of the forest. You stumble upon a tree stump which has been carved into the shape of an ancient throne. There is a dented pewter mug hanging in mid-air on a piece of a string tied to a high branch of a nearby tree. A note written on a piece of paper inside the mug says, *Welcome to the Throne of Wishes. You may make one wish at a cost of 1 Gold Piece. Drop a coin into the mug, sit down on the throne and make your wish.* If you want to pay 1 Gold Piece to make a wish, turn to **112**. If you would rather keep on walking, turn to **348**.

123

A few branches are still burning on the campfire. You are too dizzy to brandish your sword but you are able to take hold of the end of a burning branch and wave it in front of you to keep the Hippohog at bay. The Hippohog eventually gives up its attempt at eating you, and wanders off into the night. You put new wood on the fire and make sure it is burning brightly before you settle down to sleep again. You wake up very early in the morning, gather up your belongings and begin your climb of Moonstone Hills, determined to reach Skull Crag by noon. Turn to **368**.

124

Six hooded men appear from behind the trees, each of them armed with a bow and arrow pointed at you. The colour of their clothes is light and dark brown, blending in with the forest. They have long black hair and eye sockets blackened with charcoal dust. You are trapped and have to act quickly. You whisper to Hakasan to attack the three BANDITS closest to her, and you will fight the others. On the count of three you charge at the bandits. But they anticipate your move, and fire their arrows at you. If you possess a bronze shield, turn to **60**. If you do not own a shield, turn to **204**.

125

You knock gently on the iron door, trying not to attract the attention of anybody outside. Nobody comes to the door and so you tap on it sharply with a coin. Finally, after what seems like ages, you hear the lock turn and the door creak open. You are confronted by an ugly green-skinned brute of a creature with tiny eyes and tusks protruding from its thick-lipped mouth. Blocking the doorway is a Troll in black chain-mail armour, another of Lord Azzur's Imperial Guards. The Troll glares at you and says, gruffly, 'What do you want?' If you want to reply that you have been sent to torture Nicodemus, turn to **31**. If you would rather try to kick the Troll down the stairs, turn to **338**.

126

The man stops whistling and stares at you intently with one eyebrow raised higher than the other. After what seems like an age, he suddenly blurts out in a gruff voice, 'I've got bread and honey. I want copper nails to finish off building my new beehive. You got any?' If you want to trade your bag of nails for some bread and honey, turn to **268**. If you would rather politely refuse his offer and leave the square, turn to **58**.

127

You pull the cork out of the bottle with your teeth and spit it out on to the ground. You sniff the liquid inside the bottle, but it is odourless. 'Are you sure you want to drink that? I wouldn't if I were you,' Hakasan says, looking concerned. If you want to ignore her warning and drink the liquid, turn to **181**. If you want to forget the idea, you can, if you have not done so already, either eat the apples and cheese (turn to **266**) or try on the signet ring (turn to **141**). If you would rather leave now and continue on your journey to Yaztromo's Tower, turn to **383**.

128

You feel a strange tingling sensation in your legs as they start to go numb. You uncork the bottle and rub the oil into the open wound on your ankle, but snake oil does not contain any properties to counter the deadly venom. Paralysis spreads throughout your body and there is nothing you can do to stop it. Your adventure is over.

129

Mungo slaps you on the back and says, 'Good on you! I'm glad to have you on board. If you've got no other business here, it's time to go back to the *Blue Marlin*. I left a shifty-looking character guarding my boat, and you can't trust anybody in Port Blacksand. He's probably

run off with my supplies by now! Are you ready to go?'
If you want to sail to Oyster Bay with Mungo, turn to
20. If you want to change your mind, you can either join
the men playing their dice game (turn to **16**) or leave the
tavern to walk down Harbour Street towards Singing
Bridge (turn to **63**).

130

The trapdoor lifts up to reveal a narrow wooden staircase
leading down to a dark cellar. There is a very unpleasant
smell wafting up, like rotten meat. You hear the sound
of feet dragging along the floor below, and a rasping,
guttural sound like a sickly death rattle. If you want to go
down the steps to investigate, turn to **323**. If you would
rather shut the trapdoor and leave the cottage to carry on
towards Moonstone Hills, turn to **164**.

131

You manage to avoid breathing in any of the spores, and
run through the clearing holding your breath to join
Hakasan. Turn to **232**.

'My name is Hakasan Za. I am a ninja tracker from Zengis. And you?'

Reassured by the warm voice of the mystery woman, you reply that you would be willing to tell her your tale in exchange for something to eat. She agrees to your offer and tosses over a small chunk of bread, which you devour in seconds. Add 1 *STAMINA* point. You walk towards her with your hand outstretched to shake her hand. 'Stop!' she says sharply. 'There's a tripwire in front of you. I set a trap earlier. You just can't be too careful these days.' You step over the tripwire and are greeted by a friendly-looking young woman who is dressed in black robes, black cotton trousers and black leather sandals laced up over her calves. She has piercing brown eyes and long dark hair tied back in a ponytail. A two-handed curved sword is slung across her back. 'My name is Hakasan Za. I am a ninja tracker from Zengis. And you?' You tell her your name and why you came to Skull Crag, and show her the treasure map drawn by Murgat Shurr. You scoff, saying that whilst the map was accurate, the treasure, if there had been any in the first place, is long gone from the iron chest. The tracker smiles, saying, 'Oh, so it's one of Shurr's maps, is it? That charlatan makes copies of old treasure maps which are usually years out of date, and gets his minions to sell them to fools in Chalice and Port Blacksand. As you found out, they are not worth the paper they are written on. What are you going to do now?' You reply that you have no plans other than to leave Skull Crag. 'I've got no plans either. Do you want to team up to go treasure hunting?' If you want to say yes to Hakasan's proposal, turn to **81**. If you would rather politely refuse, turn to **340**.

133

'You can't fool me, I know you are in there,' the man continues. 'If you don't show yourselves before I count to five, I'm going to release poisonous gas into the room. One, two, three, four. . .' If you want to continue to keep quiet, turn to **175**. If you want to shout down to the man to say that you know he is Gurnard Jaggle and want to ask him about the puzzle box you found in Skull Crag, turn to **213**.

134

The rest of the afternoon passes without incident, and you reach the base of Moonstone Hills as the light begins to fade. You look around, very much aware that you need to find somewhere safe to spend the night. There is not a lot of choice. You can either sleep where you are in the long grass (turn to **216**) or build a bivouac out of fallen branches (turn to **250**).

135

Wondering if the pendant has magical properties, you place the chain tentatively around your neck. You are slightly disappointed that you do not feel any sudden sensation or magical powers, but are also very relieved that nothing terrible happens to you. Turn to **333**.

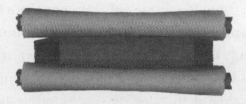

136

You walk as fast as you can, but darkness descends before you reach the shelter of Darkwood Forest. Walking by moonlight becomes frustrating as you trip over tufts of grass and rocks, and you realize you have no choice but to camp out on the open plain for the night. You find a few bits of wood and build a small fire. Hakasan shares her meagre rations of nuts and dried berries with you, which at least stops your stomach from rumbling. Add 1 *STAMINA* point. It is too dangerous for both of you to go to sleep, and you take it in turns to sleep whilst the other keeps watch. You hear sporadic grunts and growls, but the night passes without incident. You set off early next morning towards Darkwood Forest, convinced that your treasure-hunting fortunes will soon change. Turn to **56**.

137

The taller of the two bakers begins laughing nervously on hearing your question. 'Did I hear you correctly, stranger? You want us to help you climb over the wall of Hog House? Are you mad? Are you tired of life or something? Trespassers are not prosecuted – they are executed!' Will you:

Ask them again to help you climb over the wall?	Turn to **23**
Forget the idea and look at the houses?	Turn to **12**
Walk over to the shops?	Turn to **305**

138

You press forward with Hakasan at your side, bringing your swords down on the scores of Skeletons that stand in your way. As you close in on Zanbar Bone, another wave of Skeletons bears down upon you, too many for you to overcome. Exhausted and overwhelmed, you stand back-to-back with Hakasan as the Skeletons close in, their spears and swords finding their mark. You watch on in horror as Hakasan drops to the ground and is trampled underfoot; then you, too, sink to your knees under a rain of blows. The battle is lost. Your adventure is over.

You are not far from the outer edge of Darkwood Forest when Hakasan makes a sudden announcement. 'I think I've lost my appetite for treasure hunting. I can't get Horace's worrying tale out of my head. That black keystone looked very ominous to me, and so I'm going to go back to Zengis to warn our townsfolk. I'm sorry, but I'm going to say goodbye.' You try to convince her not to go, but she is having none of it. A quick hug, a smile and a wave goodbye, and she's gone, striding north-east across the plain. You walk alone towards the mighty oak trees standing tall in front of you with your mind spinning, thinking about the events of the past twenty-four hours. You see a gap in the trees where an animal path cuts through the thick undergrowth and tangled roots. You enter the forest, which is a stark mixture of light and shadow. Shafts of bright light shine down through holes in the blanket of leaves above, from where a cacophony of sound comes from the twittering birds warning the forest's inhabitants of your presence. It is not long before you reach a fork in the path. If you want to follow the right-hand path, turn to **385**. If you would prefer to take the left-hand path, turn to **87**.

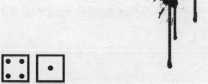

140

You are hit in the arm by an arrow. Lose 2 *STAMINA* points. If you survive, you look up to see the Wild Hill Men jumping for joy. You grit your teeth and wrench the arrow painfully out of your arm, and quickly bind the wound as best you can with a strip of cloth torn from your shirt. You watch the Wild Hill Men scrambling down the hill to attack you with their axes. You stand up to fight them one at a time.

	SKILL	STAMINA
First WILD HILL MAN	6	5
Second WILD HILL MAN	6	6

If you win, turn to **193**.

141

You slide the signet ring on to the little finger of your left hand, half expecting something terrible to happen. All your fingers tingle for a few seconds before returning to normal. You are wearing a Tyche Ring, one of the fabled rings of fortune which are made in Vatos in the Desert of Skulls. Add 2 *LUCK* points. If you have not done so already, you can either eat the apples and cheese (turn to **266**) or drink the purple liquid (turn to **127**). If you would rather leave the other items and continue your journey, turn to **383**.

142

You chase Onx, calling out his name and telling him to stop. He looks round and stops, staring at you coldly with his arms folded. You tell him that you would like to buy a bottle of healing potion after all. He is still angry, and demands 4 Gold Pieces for the potion. If you want to buy the healing potion, turn to **277**. If you think it is too much to pay for a potion and would rather set off for Darkwood Forest, turn to **7**.

143

Bignose strokes his bushy beard and eyes you a little suspiciously, saying, 'What treasure are you hoping to find in Darkwood Forest, might I ask?' If you want to reply that you are searching for gold, turn to **99**. If you want to reply that you are searching for a legendary emerald known as the Eye of the Dragon, turn to **254**.

144

You use the spare branches to make a fine crackling fire before crawling inside your bivouac. You roll out your blanket and lie down at last to rest, enjoying the warmth of the flickering flames. A full moon rises into the night sky and you stare at the bright stars, thinking about the events of the day before drifting off to sleep. You have vivid dreams and are woken up a couple of times by creature noises, but the night passes without incident. You wake up early in the morning, gather up your belongings and begin your climb of Moonstone Hills, determined to reach Skull Crag by noon. Turn to **368**.

145

You reach into your pocket and slowly count out 20 Gold Pieces, which you hand to the Trolls. 'Blimey, you must have more money than sense,' Twoteeth says, sniffing the gold coins. 'Which means you've probably got something in your backpack that we might want. So, like I said, give me your sword and let Stinkfoot look inside your backpack.' You protest, saying that you have just paid them 20 Gold Pieces to enter the palace grounds. 'I don't know what you are talking about,' Twoteeth says slyly. You have no option but to do as they say. Turn to **192**.

As you wend your way through the forest along the path, your leg catches on a razor plant, one of its sharp, blade-like fronds slicing into your flesh. You sit down on a log to bandage the wound with a piece of cloth torn from your shirt to stop the bleeding. Lose 1 *STAMINA* point. You are about to set off again when you hear the sound of rapid footsteps coming from behind. Somebody – or something – is in a hurry. Making so much noise running through the undergrowth, whoever it is certainly isn't trying to creep up on you. You stand up and see Hakasan come bounding into view, waving. 'Having a rest?' she asks jovially. You tell her about the razor plant but she isn't very sympathetic. Her expression changes, and she says in a serious voice, 'We just can't ignore what happened back there. I couldn't walk away without knowing the truth. You have to come with me to find Yaztromo. We have to warn him. He might be under attack even as we speak.' You agree that her reasoning makes perfect sense, and apologize for thinking otherwise earlier. 'Good. Deep down I knew you would come with me,' Hakasan says with a wry smile. 'Come on, we've got to go back the other way. Yaztromo lives west of here.' Turn to **2**.

147

You react too slowly. The rat's sharp teeth sink painfully into your neck. It scurries across your shoulders and tries to bite the other side of your neck, but you manage to grab hold of it and smash its head against the barrel, killing it instantly. You touch your neck and feel warm blood trickling down. Lose 1 *STAMINA* point. You suddenly hear a faint buzzing sound, and look up to see the fast-beating translucent wings and long, shiny black body of a VAMPIRE BUG diving down to attack you, its blood-sucking proboscis aiming for the wound on your neck. It is about a metre long and you must fight it.

VAMPIRE BUG   *SKILL 6*   *STAMINA 5*

If you win, turn to **121**.

148

You dive into the cornfield and wait to see who is approaching. The thundering sound of galloping hooves grows louder, and moments later you catch a glimpse of a horse's legs flashing by, heading west at full speed. Whoever it is on horseback is certainly in a hurry. You decide you might as well help yourself to some corn. Add 1 *STAMINA* point. When you have finished eating, you set off again. You estimate it will be dark by the time you reach Skull Crag, and hope you will be able to find somewhere safe to camp down for the night. Looking south, you see an old stone cottage with just the burnt edges of its thatched roof remaining, due to a fire. If you want to take a look inside the cottage, turn to **319**. If you would rather press on towards Moonstone Hills, turn to **164**.

149

You wave your merchant's pass at the thugs waiting at the top of the ramp, yelling at them to move out of the way. 'Let the merchant through!' shouts a bearded man in a black hat. You barge past the press gang to join the thronging crowd of sailors, fishermen, beggars, entertainers, and fruit and flower sellers milling about on the wharf. There are some drunken sailors standing outside the Black Lobster Tavern with their tankards in hand and arms around each other, singing loudly. If you want to go in the tavern, turn to **187**. If you want to head down Harbour Street towards Singing Bridge, turn to **63**.

150

'No!' shrieks Hakasan as the glass vial flies through the air. *Test Your Luck*. If you are Lucky, turn to **248**. If you are Unlucky, turn to **94**.

151

You both dive into the water as the pirate boat rams the flat-bottomed boat, splitting it in two. You stay underwater for as long as possible to avoid being seen, swimming as hard as you can towards the southern bank. With your lungs feeling like they are about to burst, you are forced to come to the surface to breathe in some fresh air. *Test Your Luck*. If you are Lucky, turn to **205**. If you are Unlucky, turn to **52**.

152

A weighted net flies through the air and lands on top of you both. You struggle to stand up, but cannot untangle yourself from the heavy net. You look up to see the bandits have surrounded you, and are congratulating themselves for having captured you so easily. Their leader looks down and sneers at you before turning to his fellow bandits, saying, 'These two should fetch a good price in Shazaar. Chain them up and take them away.' Alas, you will soon be sold into slavery. Your adventure is over.

153

The woman's aim is true. The heavy pot lands right on top of your head, smashing into many pieces. Lose 2 *STAMINA* points. The woman laughs and slams her bedroom window shut. Rubbing the painful lump on your head, you decide to walk over to the shops. Turn to **305**.

154

You calm Stormheart down and spur him on again, taking a detour around the back of the Skeletons. 'Zanbar Bone is here. I feel his presence,' Nicodemus shouts in your ear as you urge Stormheart on through the forest. 'There is not a moment to lose!' You ride east through the forest beyond the Skeletons, and circle back towards Yaztromo's Tower, arriving at last at a scene of despair. The tower is totally black from its base to the parapet on top. Purple vines as thick as rope burst out of the ground around the tower, climbing rapidly up the walls like fat worms. Huge numbers of Skeletons stream out of the forest and march into the clearing to line up in front of the tower. They come to a halt, standing to attention in perfect formation, fifty across and twenty deep, one thousand armed Skeletons awaiting orders. Suddenly the great oak door flies open and a figure emerges from the Tower. It is Hakasan, screaming at you to come inside. She has a look of despair in her eyes. If you want to go inside Yaztromo's Tower, turn to **279**. If you want to hack at the vines climbing the tower with your sword, turn to **115**.

155

The card sharp shakes his head and says angrily, 'No, no, no, no. I can't do that! That would be giving my secrets away. Don't be a bad loser, my friend. The hand is quicker than the eye! Trust me, you lost fairly and squarely.'

Ignoring his excuses, you reach forward and turn over the cards to see that they are all jacks! The queen of spades has vanished, no doubt deftly substituted with another jack by the sneaky card sharp. 'Well, I never! How did that happen?' he asks, laughing nervously. 'Please don't think for one moment I was trying to trick you. The queen must be here somewhere. I must have dropped it.' He fumbles anxiously in his pockets and suddenly produces a gold coin. 'Here, let me pay you for your trouble. It's a Gold Piece. Here, take it. Please. It's yours.' You think about giving him a punch in the face for trying to cheat you out of your sword, but think better of it since you have no friends in Chalice and might get set upon by the crowd. You snatch the coin from him and leave the market square. Turn to **58**.

156

After helping her out of the bear trap, you make sure Hakasan is comfortable before setting off, running as quickly as you can through the dense forest. It is not long before you come to the southern edge of Darkwood Forest and stop briefly to scan the horizon. In the far distance you can just make out the grey stone city wall surrounding Chalice. All you can see between you and Chalice is a swathe of tall grasses blowing in the wind, but there is no sign of the Chaos Warrior. If you want to carry on running south towards Chalice, turn to **200**. If you want to head west towards Catfish River, turn to **398**.

157

You spin round, realizing the rumbling noise is the sound of rock grinding against rock. You run back the way you came, peering into the gloom, arriving just in time to see a huge slab of rock sliding down from the ceiling to land on the tunnel floor with a dull thud. You try pushing against the heavy stone slab but it is a metre thick and impossible to lift or move. You give up trying, and walk back to where you were a few minutes ago. You walk on another thirty-five metres and come to a dead end. You are trapped! There is no way out of the tunnel. You are caught in a trap made by Cave Trolls, who will return in a week's time to take the possessions from your lifeless body. Your adventure is over.

158

The venom of a Yellowback is deadly, and you don't have much time to spare before your central nervous system becomes paralysed. You uncork the bottle and frantically rub the snake oil on the two red punctures on your leg where the snake bit you. Thankfully the antidote works. The pain slowly subsides, but you have a high temperature and feel very light-headed. Lose 1 *SKILL* point and 2 *STAMINA* points. Hakasan helps you stand up and you are soon able to walk normally again. Turn to **24**.

'Friend or foe?' he asks in a booming voice

159

You walk towards where the sound of the voice is coming from and enter a small clearing where you see a short, stocky man with balding hair and a long bushy beard sitting on a log, sharpening his battleaxe. He is wearing a chain-mail shirt over his tunic, a cloak and big brown boots. By his side are a crossbow and an iron-rimmed wooden shield. He doesn't seem concerned by your sudden appearance. 'Friend or foe?' he asks in a booming voice. If you want to reply 'friend', turn to **360**. If you want to reply 'foe', turn to **209**.

160

You are in a deep sleep when a huge SCORPION BUG emerges from its nearby borehole. Virtually blind, Scorpion Bugs detect even the slightest vibrations on the surface above ground. Attracted by your breathing, it crawls out of its hole to inject you with the paralysis-inducing sting at the end of its plated exoskeleton body. You wake up just as it tries to snare you with its sharp pincer-like claws to drag you down into its borehole to feed on you. Although you still feel exhausted from the effects of the Tick-Tick virus, you must fight the Scorpion Bug. Lose 1 *SKILL* point and 2 *STAMINA* points before combat begins.

SCORPION BUG   SKILL 8   STAMINA 10

If you win, turn to **388**.

161

The lid of the box lifts up easily to reveal two large fangs, certainly large enough to be dragon's teeth. You put them in your pocket and open the drawer fully to see if it contains anything else. Turn to **189**.

162

You rub the orange wax over the open wound on your ankle. You feel a tingling sensation in your legs, but the uncomfortable feeling quickly subsides as the stikkle wax neutralizes the toxic venom. Breathing a sigh of relief, you carry on down the tunnel and soon arrive at another junction. If you want to go left, turn to **197**. If you want to go right, turn to **292**.

163

A quick search of the robbers yields 3 Copper Pieces and a black pearl. You carry on down Thread Street, where you see four armed guards marching towards you. You see a narrow alleyway almost hidden from view in shadows on your left, which you slip down unnoticed. It ends at a T-junction where you turn right into Palace Street. Turn to **371**.

164

Walking through the tall grasses of the Eastern Plain, you see the great expanse of the Moonstone Hills looming before you, with the foothills no more than half a day's walk away. To your left, the plain stretches north as far as you can see all the way to Darkwood Forest, and to the south all the way to Silver River and beyond. You walk on determinedly, but looking at your map, you have a lingering doubt about its authenticity. Half an hour later, you see a flock of birds high in the sky circling above a building about half a kilometre north-eastwards. If you want to investigate, turn to **71**. If you would rather keep heading east, turn to **134**.

165

Bignose's mouth drops open in disbelief as you recount Horace Wolff's tragic story. 'Oh my goodness, that is the most terrible news I've heard since the disappearance of Bigleg! I would like to come with you to Yaztromo's, but I have to find my cousin. The good news is that you are not far from the wizard's tower. Half an hour's walk this way,' he says, pointing over his shoulder with his thumb. 'If there is anything of mine that might be of use to you, please say. I would happily trade.' If you possess a Rune Ring, turn to **27**. If you do not own this ring, turn to **235**.

166

The urchin pockets the Copper Piece and runs off. You soon find out that he was not telling the truth. As you smear the blood on your arm it starts to burn like acid. The pain is severe as the toxic blood begins to eat through your skin. Ignoring the rank smell coming from the barrel, you reach in and grab a sodden rag, wiping your arm frantically with it. The water quickly neutralizes the acidic blood, but not without loss to your health. Lose 1 *SKILL* point and 3 *STAMINA* points. You toss the rag aside and walk on to the T-junction. Turn to **206**.

167

Without weapons, there is not much that you can do to defeat the bandits, so you decide to run for it. Turn to **152**.

168

You are not even halfway across the square when the guards snap out of their frozen state and pour out through the palace gates to give chase. You hear the twanging sound of crossbows being fired, and one of the bolts finds its mark in the middle of your back. Your adventure is over.

169

You head down the narrow right-hand tunnel for thirty

metres, the light from your lantern casting eerie shadows on the rough-hewn tunnel wall. Suddenly you hear a dull rumbling sound coming from behind you. Turn to **157**.

170

Onx looks at you with a face like thunder. He's very annoyed that you won't help him, especially since he helped save you from getting captured by the pirates. He becomes more and more agitated, and starts shouting and blaming you for his boat being sunk by the pirates. He starts talking in a strange language, his voice getting increasingly loud. He picks up a handful of dirt and throws it at you, and makes a rapid, sweeping gesture in the air with his other hand. You have been cursed! Lose 2 *SKILL* points and 1 *LUCK* point. He turns and runs off at a fast pace towards Largo. If you want to change your mind and run after Onx to buy the healing potion, turn to **142**. If you would rather let him go and set off for Darkwood Forest, turn to **47**.

171

As you reach for your sword, the Cyclops lets out a deafening roar and reaches over the counter to grab you by the throat with its huge hand. You try to pull its hand away, but the enraged creature's overpowering strength is far greater than yours. You pass out and never wake up. Your adventure is over.

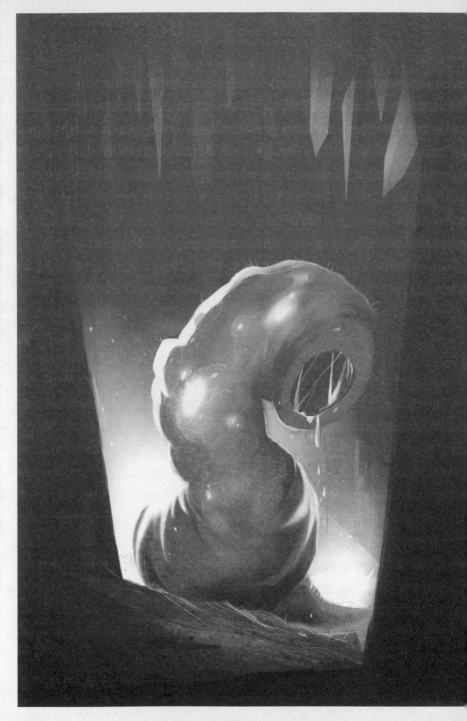

The bloated jelly-like worm flops down on to the cave floor with a dull spla

172

The venom of a Yellowback is quick-acting, and you don't have much time to spare. You uncork the bottle and rub the oil on the two red punctures on your leg where the snake bit you. Unfortunately skunk oil is not an antidote for snake bites. Your temperature rises and your heart starts pounding in your chest as paralysis of your central nervous system sets in. Hakasan tries to help, frantically trying to bleed the poison from the snake-bite wound, but there is nothing she can do to save you. It's not long before you lose consciousness, never to recover. Your adventure is over.

173

Bignose looks at you disdainfully, and says, 'Never mind. I'll tell Mariola that her husband's ring has been found but is now in the possession of a selfish oaf. Now, I've got better things to do than stand here talking to the likes of you. I need to find my second cousin, so I'll be on my way. Cheerio!' The Dwarf barges past you, humming loudly to himself, and is soon out of sight. Turn to **246**.

174

A huge semi-transparent, gelatinous worm with pulsating innards which produce a luminescent green glow starts to slide down through the hole. It's a flesh-eating GIANT LAVAWORM, a deadly creature and scourge of the Cave Trolls. The bloated jelly-like worm flops down on to the cave floor with a dull splat. It has powerful sonar senses for echolocation, and slithers towards you, intent on dissolving you with its acidic mucous secretion and feeding on your liquid remains. You must fight it. Normal edged weapons have little effect on Lavaworms. If you possess a pouch of salt, turn to **21**. If you do not have any salt, you must fight the Lavaworm with your sword. Turn to **336**.

175

A small glass vial flies up through the trapdoor and shatters on impact with the floor to release a cloud of green gas from the broken glass. The gas spirals towards you, enveloping you and making you choke. Gasping for air, you climb down the rope ladder as fast as you can, but cannot escape the encircling cloud of poisonous gas. You drop to your knees, clutching your throat, and fall unconscious. Your adventure is over.

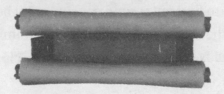

176

You put your index finger to your lips, motioning to Hakasan to keep quiet. Walking as quietly as possible, you take a short detour on your trek to Yaztromo's Tower. Turn to **246**.

177

You soon arrive at the lair of the slain Norgul, where its cauldron is still bubbling away, suspended above the dying embers of the fire. You walk through the lair and soon arrive at another junction. If you want to go left, turn to **28**. If you want to go straight on, turn to **316**.

178

There are five streets to choose from – River Street, Palace Street, Temple Street, Market Street and Thread Street. You discount River Street since it is unlikely the guards would take Nicodemus back over the river, and also Market Street, as it only leads to the main gates. Temple Street is blocked by a stack of handcarts belonging to market porters who are waving placards in protest against low wages, which leaves a choice of two streets. If you want to go down Palace Street, turn to **371**. If you want to go down Thread Street, turn to **80**.

179

A search of the Ogre yields 5 Copper Pieces and an iron key which it was wearing around its neck on a piece of string. You pocket the coins and the key, and turn to the timber yard owner, who steps backwards, afraid that you might attack him. He apologizes profusely and begs you not to harm him, offering you 10 Copper Pieces and 3 Gold Pieces in payment for having treated you so badly. You snatch the coins from him and walk back down Armoury Lane to the market square and on to Beggar's Alley. Turn to **283**. Or, if you have not done so already, you may go back to the market square to go to Silver Street. Turn to **104**.

180

You pocket the merchant's pass and hand 10 Gold Pieces to Cris before stepping into the small rowing boat laden with wicker baskets. Dod pushes the boat out into the river, saying, 'Moor up at Lobster Wharf. It's very crowded there and nobody will be bothered about you. But don't come back here without my boat. Remember I've got your horse! No boat, no horse. Do we have an understanding?' You nod your head in agreement, smiling, and wave goodbye, reminding Cris to feed and water Stormheart whilst you're away. Turn to **395**.

181

You place the bottle to your lips, hesitating for a second before gulping down the liquid. You feel a warm glow in your throat which spreads down into your stomach. You have drunk a Potion of Strength. Add 2 *SKILL* points, 3 *STAMINA* points and 1 *LUCK* point. With a smug grin on your face, you apologize insincerely to Hakasan for drinking it all. If you have not done so already, you may either eat the apples and cheese (turn to **266**) or try on the signet ring (turn to **141**). If you would rather leave these items behind and continue on your journey, turn to **383**.

182

You are unable to dive out of the way in time. The massive boulder hurtles down and crashes into you with fatal impact. Your adventure is over.

183

You are engulfed by a swarm of flying insects which bite and sting you all over. You can hardly see a thing, and swiping at them with your sword is pointless. Lose 4 *STAMINA* points and 1 *SKILL* point. If you are still alive, you are relieved to see Yaztromo come to your aid, blasting the insects with a Volcano Spell which makes them all explode, showering the Skeleton horde with insect fragments. Zanbar Bone rages from his throne, and commands his tentacled beast to attack. Turn to **11**.

184

The man smiles, turning over the card to reveal a jack of hearts. 'Hard luck, stranger,' he says hollowly. 'I'm afraid you failed to find the lady. Your sword, please.' If you want to hand over your sword, turn to **4**. If you want to ask him to turn over the queen of spades card before handing over your sword, turn to **155**.

185

Hakasan comes bounding into view with a frown across her face. 'No rabbits, I'm afraid,' she says disconsolately. 'Looks like it's going to be nuts and dry berries again tonight.' Hakasan shares her meagre rations with you, which at least stops your stomach from rumbling. Add 1 *STAMINA* point. You stoke the fire before retiring to the pigpen, taking it in turns to sleep whilst the other keeps watch. You hear sporadic grunts and growls from outside, but the night passes without incident. You set off early next morning towards Darkwood Forest, convinced that your treasure-hunting fortunes will soon change. Turn to **56**.

186

You put the wooden box on the ground and swing your sword down hard on it, cleaving it in two. You notice a small lead ball roll out of the box at the same time as a cloud of green gas escapes from a glass vial that is shattered by your sword. The gas envelops you, making you choke. You run out of the cave and down the tunnel, gasping for air, but cannot escape the poisonous gas cloud. You drop to your knees clutching your mouth, and fall unconscious. Your adventure is over.

Behind the wooden bar stands a stern-looking man

The Black Lobster Tavern is like any other tavern in Port Blacksand where the ale flows freely. Everybody is on the make. Slippery-tongued rogues with multiple tattoos, slicked-back hair and darting eyes sell worthless treasure maps to gullible customers. Smiling charlatans with flowing locks sell dyed water as potions of strength. Sly-looking crooks take good money from would-be fortune hunters in payment for blunt swords sold as magic dragon-slaying weapons. And sly thieves simply steal money and purses from their victims when the chance comes. You open the large oak door and are met by a waft of stale air and a cacophony of noise from the drunken sailors, boat builders, fishermen and fish-market workers packed into the dimly lit tavern, sloshing down mugs of ale and bragging loudly about their seafaring adventures. Behind the wooden bar stands a stern-looking man wearing a dirty apron over his white vest. He has gold earrings in both ears, and his chest and arms are covered in tattoos. There is a sign above the bar which says *Sail in a gale with Armpit Ale*. The innkeeper eyes you suspiciously as you approach the bar. In the far corner of the tavern you catch sight of two men sitting at a table rolling dice with a lot of noisy enthusiasm. If you want to talk to the innkeeper, turn to **317**. If you want to join the men playing their dice game, turn to **16**.

188

The wall is some four metres high and made of smooth stone; there is nothing to take hold of to climb up. You look down the street and see two men walking towards you in white hats and aprons, their faces dusted with flour. They are bakers, and look very tired from kneading heavy dough and baking bread since dawn. Will you:

Ask the bakers to help lift you over the wall?   Turn to **137**

Forget the idea and look at the houses?   Turn to **12**

Have a look at the shops?   Turn to **305**

189

You find a jar and a bandage at the back of the drawer. The words *Cure-all – do not eat* are scribbled on the label of the jar. You uncork the jar to find it contains a small amount of yellow paste at the bottom which smells like rotten eggs. Will you:

Eat some of the paste?   Turn to **35**

Rub a small amount of paste on a wound?   Turn to **103**

Take the jar and bandage back to Hakasan?   Turn to **325**

190

Hakasan stares at you coldly and says, 'I'm not so sure. How did he know so much about Zanbar Bone? And how do you explain the keystone? But as you wish. Let's get him buried and be on our way. Poor man, what a terrible way to end his life.' You find a long branch to use as a lever to lift up the block of granite, enough to pull poor Horace out from underneath. You bury him and mark his grave with a small pile of stones with Hakasan notably silent throughout, lost in solemn thought. 'So where should we go to now?' she asks without much enthusiasm in her voice. If you want to say you should keep on walking towards Darkwood Forest, turn to **139**. If you want to suggest that you head west, turn to **342**.

191

The little old man lets out a huge cheer as you dispatch the last of the Blue Imps. 'Wonderful! Wonderful!' he shouts out happily at the top of his voice. 'I'm saved! I'm saved!' You untie the ropes binding him to the post and he starts jumping in the air with excitement. You ask him how he ended up becoming a human scarecrow. 'Those damned Imps,' he says angrily. 'I was on my way to Deedle Water a week ago, and had camped down for the night. I was asleep when they crept into my camp and kidnapped me. They bound my wrists and ankles and brought me here hanging from a pole carried by two of the little rascals. That was not an enjoyable experience, I can tell you. They are so short, I kept bumping my head on the ground! Well, it only got worse, didn't it? They plonked me here in the middle of their blueberry bushes and said that unless I scared the birds away, they would eat me! Carnivores, that's what they are! Can you imagine those horrible little creatures with their knives and forks slicing me up? There's hardly any meat on me! Why would they bother? They'd be better off eating the blooming blueberries, but they don't. They grow blueberries just to make a special dye which they rub on their skin to make it turn blue. I love eating blueberries myself. Which reminds me – I'm starving!'

The old man begins cramming handful after handful of blueberries into his mouth. You follow his lead and gorge on the tasty berries until you can't eat any more. Add 2 *STAMINA* points. Finally he lets out a satisfied, loud burp and asks you where you are headed, and you reply that you are on your way to Moonstone Hills on a quest. He lets out a low whistle, and says, 'Well, a bit of advice for you, then, before I go. If you are thinking of sleeping out here on the plain, make sure you build a fire to keep away the hungry critters roaming around at night. And since you are going to be exploring caves, here's a lump of stikkle wax in case you get bitten by a Gronk. Just rub it on the bite and you'll be fine. Now I must be on my way to Deedle Water. My wife will be wondering what happened to me.' He shakes your hand and wishes you luck. You watch him gather up some blueberries before heading off. If you want to look inside the Blue Imps' cabin, turn to **38**. If you would rather carry on to Moonstone Hills, turn to **134**.

192

You hand your weapons over to Twoteeth, and take off your backpack to let Stinkfoot look inside. 'Thank you,' Twoteeth says insincerely. 'You can go now. We'll look after your things, won't we, Stinkfoot? That will teach you to try and trick your way into Lord Azzur's palace. Go on, beat it.' You complain vociferously, but the Trolls insist that you leave, and threaten you with jail if you don't. Complaining is futile, and there is nothing you can do to stop them sharing out your weapons and belongings between them. You have lost everything except for your jewellery and the items in your pockets. Lose 2 *LUCK* points and 2 *SKILL* points. The only hope you have in gaining entry to the palace is to walk over to the lone guard standing on the corner of Palace Street, knock him out to take his armour and weapons, and try to enter the palace disguised as a guard. Turn to **59**.

193

You empty the Wild Hill Men's leather shoulder bags on to the ground and find a small pig carved out of stone, 2 Gold Pieces, a small box of fish hooks, a piece of flint and a small bag of salt. You take the items you want, and also a small hand axe, a bow and six arrows. Pleased with your haul, you set off again. Turn to **345**.

194

Whilst she is resting, you take the opportunity to pick some ripe berries from nearby bushes, which you share with Hakasan. Add 1 *STAMINA* point. Feeling better, Hakasan stands up, and you set off again. A few minutes later, you hear somebody in the distance call out, 'Bigleg! Bigleg! Where are you?' If you want to see who is calling out, turn to **159**. If you want to keep quiet and avoid whoever it is, turn to **176**.

195

Ten Gold Pieces seems like a lot of money to pay for a dagger, but Cy assures you that not only will the dagger fly true when thrown, its blade, which is made of the finest Salamonian steel, is guaranteed to pierce almost anything. You hand 10 Gold Pieces to the Cyclops and place the dagger in your belt. Add 1 *SKILL* point. There is nothing else that you can afford to buy, so you leave the shop and walk to the end of Armoury Lane. Turn to **33**.

196

The pendant lies unseen in the undergrowth as you set off in the direction Bignose suggested. Turn to **333**.

197

You head down the narrow left-hand tunnel for thirty metres wondering where the passage might lead to. Suddenly you hear a dull rumbling sound coming from behind you. Turn to **157**.

198

Nicodemus calls to you, saying he is running out of energy and will only be able to keep Zanbar Bone in place for a few seconds more. Yaztromo is breathing hard, exhausted from casting spells, and it is all Hakasan can do to stop the front row of Skeletons from breaking through. You grab the flintlock pistol from your belt, take aim at the Demon Prince's skull, and pull the trigger. There is a puff of smoke as the black powder ignites in the gun barrel with a bang, shooting out the lead ball. Roll two dice. If the number rolled is equal to or less than your *SKILL* score, turn to **267**. If the number rolled is greater than your *SKILL* score, turn to **119**.

199

Your sword finds its mark, sinking into your attacker's shoulder with a dull thud. It makes a gurgling sound in its throat but increases its grip on your ankle. The creature shuffles into the shaft of light shining down from the room above, and you see it has pallid grey skin covered with festering sores. Its gaping mouth is torn away on one side to reveal broken black teeth and a lolling tongue, and its sunken eyes are red-rimmed and lifeless. Oblivious to the gaping wound in its shoulder, the ZOMBIE lurches forward trying to bite you. You must fight the undead creature.

ZOMBIE   *SKILL* 6   *STAMINA* 5

If you win, turn to **67**.

200

You run through the tall grasses without stopping until you can run no further. Lose 1 *STAMINA* point. You are exhausted and have to pause to get your breath back. Chalice is less than a kilometre away and there is still no sign of the Chaos Warrior. To your left is the vast field of ripe corn and before you stands a farmhouse. You see a man come out of the farmhouse and climb into the driver's seat of a loaded cart tethered to a grey horse. The man cracks his whip and the horse sets off at a fast trot, heading in your direction. If you want to call out to the man to ask if he has seen Klash, turn to **91**. If you would rather watch him drive by without saying anything, turn to **260**.

201

You try to turn the brass handle, but the door is firmly locked. If you want to pull the cord to ring the doorbell, turn to **97**. If you would rather leave Hog House, turn to **30**.

202

The monstrous creature lumbers forward, its tentacles curling in and out of its cavernous mouth, trying to snare you. Its iron-like hide is difficult to pierce with normal weapons, and its swirling tentacles make it difficult to fight. You must reduce your Attack Strength by 4 points during each Attack Round.

QUAG-SHUGGUTH   *SKILL 12*   *STAMINA 13*

If you win, turn to **362**.

203

You walk down the narrow tunnel some forty metres, the light from your lantern casting eerie shadows against the rock wall. Suddenly you hear a dull rumbling sound coming from behind you. Turn to **157**.

204

You dive sideways, trying to avoid being hit by the arrows. Roll two dice. If the number rolled is less than or equal to your *SKILL* score, turn to **3**. If the number rolled is greater than your *SKILL* score, turn to **364**.

205

Luckily for you, the pirates are looking in the other direction when you surface. You breathe in a lungful of fresh air and dive down again to continue swimming underwater. You see reeds in front of you in the murky water, and swim towards them so that you can surface hidden from view. When you reach the reeds you find Onx is already there. He hands you a reed and whispers to you to keep your head under the water and breathe through the reed. You wait ten minutes before surfacing again to find that the pirates have gone. You climb out of the river and begin the walk back to Largo. Onx is very upset that his boat was sunk by the pirates. He says a new boat will cost him 10 Gold Pieces to have made, and offers to sell you a bottle of healing potion for 2 Gold Pieces to help pay for it. If you want to buy the healing potion, turn to **18**. If would rather decline his offer, turn to **170**.

206

Lion Street is cobbled, and much wider and brighter than Beggar's Alley. It certainly looks to be in a more affluent part of the town. On the opposite side, a high wall runs the length of the street. There are stone gargoyles fixed to the top of the wall every ten metres or so, staring down threateningly at all who might pass by. Above the wall you can just see the top floor and roof of a large mansion house. Whoever lives there obviously wants privacy and does not welcome visitors. On the near side of the street there are a few shops to your right and houses to your left. Will you:

Try to climb over the wall of the mansion house?	Turn to **188**
Take a look at the houses?	Turn to **12**
Look in the shop windows?	Turn to **305**

207

After paying your entry fee, the guard calls for the main gates to open. As you pass through the gates, you are suddenly grabbed by four other guards and pulled off your horse. Before you have time to react, iron shackles are clamped on your wrists and you are led off to the guardhouse nearby and thrown in the cells downstairs. You rattle the cell bars in anger, demanding to know why you have been put in jail. One of the guards looks coldly at you, and says, 'You shouldn't steal people's horses. You probably thought you were going to get a good price for it here, didn't you? Tell that to Lord Azzur. If you escape with your head, you'll be lucky. You'll more likely end up on Gallows Hill.' With that he turns and walks upstairs. You call out to him, protesting your innocence, but your words fall on deaf ears. Your adventure is over.

208

Flashing your sword swiftly through the air, you survive the battle unscathed. Add 1 *LUCK* point. Breathing a sigh of relief, you carry on down the tunnel and soon arrive at another junction. If you want to go left, turn to **197**. If you want to go right, turn to **292**.

209

The DWARF jumps up and grabs his shield, and runs at you swinging his battleaxe, yelling a war cry at the top of his voice.

DWARF   *SKILL 7*   *STAMINA 7*

If you win, turn to **381**.

210

You empty the Man-Orc's pouch to find a piece of chalk, some dried nettles and a tiny cast-iron pig trinket. If you want to go back down into the cellar to examine the crack in the wall, turn to **244**. If you would rather leave the cottage to carry on towards Moonstone Hills, turn to **164**.

211

You warn the urchin that you will come back and find him if the information you are paying for is false. 'I saw them! Honestly I did. It was the funny old wizard who lives under the bridge who was being dragged through the square by two of Lord Azzur's Imperial Guards. They were Trolls! Nobody dared challenge them. They barged through the crowd and disappeared down Palace Street,' the boy says convincingly. You give the boy 1 Gold Piece and decide which way to go. If you believe the urchin and want to go down Palace Street, turn to **371**. If you want to go down one of the other streets, turn to **178**.

An old man pops his head through the trap door and looks at you suspiciousl

212

Although you're excited by the thought of having finally reached your goal, you approach the iron chest with caution. Much to your surprise, there is no lock on the chest. Sensing a trap, you lift the lid with the tip of your sword, and cannot believe your eyes when you do. Apart from a small wooden box inside, the chest is empty! Somebody has beaten you to it. You curse loudly and kick the chest in anger, which sends it spinning across the cave floor. The wooden box falls out, and you pick it up to see that it is made of polished mahogany and has an ornately carved lid with a beetle motif in its centre. You shake the box and hear something rattle inside. Inspecting it closely, you see that the lid is tight-fitting. If you want to open it, turn to **307**. If you would rather put the box in your backpack without opening it, turn to **389**.

213

An old man pops his head through the trapdoor and looks at you suspiciously. He has thinning white hair and is wearing a sleeveless jacket over his dark green shirt. He climbs up the ladder and steps into the room, keeping his eyes on you, a glass vial held threateningly in one hand. 'Don't even think about it,' the man says coldly, gesturing towards your drawn sword. 'Put your weapons away so we can talk. You are right, I am Gurnard Jaggle. I would be willing to tell you about my puzzle boxes, but the information will cost you 3 Gold Pieces.' If you want to pay his price for information about the wooden box, turn to **108**. If you would rather tell him you are going to leave his tree house and continue on your journey, turn to **29**.

214

The old man quickly shakes your hand, eager to close the deal. He's clearly very pleased with his purchase. You put the 10 Gold Pieces in your pocket and casually ask who Gurnard Jaggle might be. 'He is my brother! He is a very talented man, but he was robbed of the only treasure he ever found and that made him bitter and twisted. He started doing some bad things and disappeared a few months ago. It's all very sad. Anyway, I'm closing my shop for thirty minutes, so I'm going to have to ask you to leave.' A sideways glance at Crusha shows that he means business. You bid Jethro Jaggle farewell and leave his shop to walk to the end of the street. Turn to **82**.

215

As soon as you have finished your breakfast, Yaztromo hands you 15 Gold Pieces and tells you to get ready to depart. You meet him on the ground floor, where he asks you to touch the tips of the fingers of your fighting arm with the fingertips of his opposite hand. A bolt of energy suddenly shoots up your arm and you immediately feel incredibly dexterous and powerful. Increase your *SKILL* score to 12. Turn to **272**.

You rummage through your backpack and find a few scraps of food to eat. Add 1 *STAMINA* point. It is a cool evening and so you decide to make a campfire. You roll out your blanket and lie down with your sword nearby for comfort, to enjoy the warmth of the flickering flames. A full moon rises in the night sky and you stare at the bright stars, thinking about the events of the day before eventually drifting off to sleep. You have not been asleep for long when you are woken by some snuffling sounds. You jump up, grab your sword and peer into the half-light looking for movement. Suddenly you see something. It's a large, round black shape and it is coming slowly towards you on four stumpy legs, its snuffling sounds getting louder and louder. A cloud that was partially blocking out the moon drifts away and you see the creature in front of you in the moonlight. It has a huge head with an enormous tusked mouth, wide snout, tiny eyes and ears, and a thick-set neck that joins its head to its bulbous body covered with thick grey hide. Its keen sense of smell has led the HIPPOHOG to you, looking for its evening meal. On seeing you, the Hippohog breaks wind, releasing a stench that is so rancid that it makes you retch and feel light-headed. Hippohogs overcome their prey by first disabling them with their acrid intestinal gas before trampling them underfoot. But they are also afraid of fire. *Test Your Luck*. If you are Lucky, turn to **123**. If you are Unlucky, turn to **278**.

217

You unwittingly step on a snake which was bathing in the warm early morning sunshine. It rears up on its tail, coiled like a spring, and strikes at lightning speed, sinking its fangs into your leg to inject toxic venom into your veins. It slithers off quickly into the undergrowth. It has distinctive black zigzag markings running the length of its yellow back, leaving you in no doubt that you have been bitten by a deadly YELLOWBACK SNAKE. Your leg immediately goes numb and starts to swell up, and you drop to the ground, rolling around in agony. If you took a bottle of oil from a street-sweeper in Chalice, turn to **10**. If you do not have a bottle, turn to **332**.

218

You put the pendant in your back pocket, not realizing that there is a hole in it. It falls out through the hole and disappears into the undergrowth. *Test Your Luck*. If you are Lucky, turn to **320**. If you are Unlucky, turn to **196**.

219

You walk across the beautifully manicured lawn and up the marble steps to the formidable shiny black front door. A cord with a brass knob at the end hang downs to your left. If you want to pull the cord to ring the doorbell, turn to **97**. If you would rather try opening the door, turn to **201**.

220

The bandits are excellent bowmen, and before you are able to reach cover, more arrows thud into your body. Roll one die. This is the number of arrows that strike you, with the minimum number being two. Lose 2 *STAMINA* points for each arrow that finds its mark. If you are still alive, turn to **312**.

221

Your rowing boat is met by hail of crossbow bolts, some bolts lodging into the hull and others flying overhead, but none hit you. Nicodemus mutters more arcane words, creating an invisible shield which is only noticeable when you see crossbow bolts deflecting off it to land harmlessly in the river. You pass under the arch of the city wall, rowing away from Port Blacksand as fast as you can. With nobody in pursuit, you settle down to row steadily upriver, discussing the threat of Zanbar Bone. Turn to **379**.

222

The dagger misses its target, flying harmlessly past the Demon's skull. Unable to hold back the Skeleton horde any longer, Hakasan is pushed to the ground and trampled underfoot. Before you can draw your sword, the Skeletons are on top of you, their spears and swords piercing your flesh. You sink to your knees, defeated. Your adventure is over.

Onx dives into the water and swims to the bank as the pirate boat rams your boat, splitting it in two. You are thrown into the fast-flowing river with the oarsmen plunging their oars into the water to strike you. You are caught on the side of the head by one of the oars, which knocks you out. The pirates grab hold of you and haul you into their boat. You wake up to find that they have taken all of your possessions, including your sword. They chain your ankle to the bench seat in the boat and give you an oar. 'Welcome aboard,' says the sneering captain. 'You are now officially under the command of Captain Crow. Row hard and you might get fed.' You try to convince the captain about the imminent return of Zanbar Bone, but he tells you to stop making up fanciful stories and concentrate on rowing. Wondering about the fate of poor Hakasan, you begin your new life as a river pirate. Your adventure is over.

You hear a loud screech overhead, and look up to see a giant winged reptile with a long tail diving straight down towards you. Its scaly skin is bronze in colour, and it has a long head with an elongated jaw housing rows of needle-sharp teeth. Before you have time to draw your sword, the TERROSAUR strikes, sinking its sharp claws into your arm and swooping back up into the sky with you in tow. The pain is unbearable. You try to wriggle free but give up when you see you are too high in the sky to risk falling to the ground. The screeching reptile heads west at speed, flying over the Moonstone Hills towards the foreboding line of giant trees which marks the edge of Darkwood Forest. Banking to the right, it glides north over the high treetops and beyond, crossing Red River and the Pagan Plains towards the solitary peak of Firetop Mountain. As you close in on the red-topped mountain, you see a large nest built on a rocky ledge halfway up. The Terrosaur circles the nest, calling out with high-pitched screeches to two hatchlings which are excitedly flapping their leathery wings. You realize that you are going to be their next meal. There is nothing you can do to stop the giant reptile gliding down to its nest to feed you to its offspring. Your adventure is over.

An enormous troll's head some five metres high
carved out of the face of a rocky outcrop

225

The undergrowth thins out a little, allowing you to make better progress. You keep going until you reach a clearing where you see an enormous Troll's head some five metres high carved out of the face of a rocky outcrop. The idol is partly concealed by moss and vegetation, and has stone steps leading up to its open mouth, which is nearly two metres in diameter. If you want to walk into the open mouth of the idol, turn to **37**. If you want to keep on walking, turn to **284**.

226

The Blue Imps may be small in height, but they are very quick and dexterous. Fight them one at a time.

	SKILL	STAMINA
First BLUE IMP	6	5
Second BLUE IMP	6	4
Third BLUE IMP	6	5

If you win, turn to **191**.

227

A quick search of the Dark Elves' pockets yields 1 Gold Piece, 2 Copper Pieces, and a small silver box containing a silver key. You put the items in your backpack and take one of the serrated knives for good luck. You climb back on to Stormheart and ride off again, determined not to stop again for any reason. Turn to **66**.

228

There is no sign of life. The main farmhouse building is in total ruin, but there is a wooden pigpen at the back which remains standing. You open the hatch and your nostrils are met by a ripe, fruity aroma which makes you cough. But at least the pigpen is dry inside, has a roof and four walls, and should keep out unwanted creatures of the night. Hakasan says she is going to try to catch a rabbit for supper in the dying light of the day. You wish her luck and build a fire using the wood from a broken table you find in the ruins. With the fire lit, you rummage around the ruins and find a pair of dirty old leather boots inside a wooden box hidden under some rubble. They appear to be your size. If you want to try on the boots, turn to **393**. If you would rather leave them in the box, turn to **98**.

229

The Man-Orcs have leather pouches on their belts which you empty out on to the floor. You find a Copper Piece, seven teeth, a silver button, a glass eye, an arrowhead and three polished stones. After taking what you want, you look round the room to see if there is anything else which might be of use to you. There are five jars on a shelf containing rats' tails, small bones, worms, dead flies and sheep's eyeballs. You have room in your backpack for one jar, but if you want to take more, you will have to leave something behind for each additional jar you take. In the far corner of the room, you discover a wooden trapdoor partly hidden by an old iron stove. If you want to move the stove to unbolt the trapdoor, turn to **130**. If you would rather leave the cottage and carry on towards Moonstone Hills, turn to **164**.

230

You put the first of the twenty brass keys into the lock, but it fails to unlock the door. Your luck changes with the eighth key you try, and you hear a satisfying click as the lock turns in the door. You pull on the door, which creaks open on its rusty hinges. The stone steps lead down to a cold and gloomy corridor below, which is lit by oil lamps suspended from the ceiling. You walk slowly down the steps, trying not to make any noise, and soon arrive at a junction. You hear the sound of footsteps coming down the left side of the corridor, and decide to investigate. Turn to **295**.

231

A search of the Norgul's lair reveals a string purse hidden in a small recess in the wall. You untie the purse and find that it contains 5 Gold Pieces. Add 1 *LUCK* point. You place the purse in your backpack and walk over to the tunnel at the back of the Norgul's lair and soon arrive at another junction. If you want to go left, turn to **46**. If you want to go right, turn to **111**.

232

You run through the clearing, holding your breath, to where Hakasan is waiting for you. 'That was the most hideous thing I have ever seen in Darkwood Forest,' she says with disgust. You carry on heading west, and progress becomes easier as the undergrowth thins out. Walking along, it dawns on you that all the birds and creatures have gone quiet, and you comment on the fact to Hakasan. 'Something must have spooked them,' Hakasan says, drawing her sword. You stand still, listening out for any noises. 'What's that?' asks Hakasan. You concentrate hard, and hear faint rustling sounds coming from the left, and then from the right. You tell Hakasan to stand back-to-back with you and be ready to challenge whoever is approaching. You do not have to wait long to find out who it is. 'Put down your swords. Put down your backpacks. And walk back the way you came. There are six arrows pointed at you. You have ten seconds to make up your mind,' a man's deep voice commands coldly. If you want to obey the unseen man, turn to **377**. If you want to stand your ground, turn to **124**.

233

Hakasan agrees with your decision, saying, 'We need to get to Yaztromo's Tower before dark or we could be in for a very challenging night in Darkwood Forest!' Turn to **225**.

234

Hanging on to the top of the wall, you ease yourself down as far as you can. With your legs dangling down, you drop to the ground below, twisting your ankle badly as you land. Lose 1 *SKILL* point and 1 *STAMINA* point. You are annoyed at yourself for getting injured unnecessarily. You look both ways down the street and decide what to do. If you want to look at the houses, turn to **12**. If you want to walk over to the shops, turn to **305**.

235

You tell Bignose that you do not have many items to barter with, but say you would like his battleaxe if a deal could be done for it. If you want to offer him your goblet with the unicorn-head motif and brass bell in exchange for his battleaxe, turn to **120**. If you would rather offer him your brass bell and candle for it, turn to **344**.

236

Clambering up and down hills, over boulders, rocks, stones and shale all morning is very tiring and thirsty work. You slip over several times, hurting your arm in one particularly bad fall. Lose 1 *STAMINA* point. You push on, reaching a narrow gully between two steep hills through which a stream is gently running. If you want to stop to fill up your water flask, turn to **95**. If you would rather keep on walking east, turn to **345**.

237

Roll two dice, and add 4 to the total if you are using Lucky Bones. If the number is 8 or higher, turn to **75**. If the total is 7 or less, turn to **366**.

238

Hakasan nods her head in agreement and says, 'If it is true, this news about Zanbar Bone is very grim. It is fortunate that we are close to Darkwood Forest. We should go to Yaztromo's Tower without further delay. We have to warn him. He might be under attack even as we speak. Let's bury the stonemason and be on our way.' You find a long branch to use as a lever to lift up the block of granite, enough to pull Horace's body out from underneath. You bury him and mark his grave with a small pile of stones. You set off towards the wall of oak trees standing tall ahead. Your mind is spinning, thinking about the events of the past twenty-four hours. You see a gap in the trees where an animal path cuts through the thick undergrowth and tangled roots. You enter the forest, which is a stark mixture of light and shadow. Shafts of bright light shine down through holes in the heavy blanket of leaves above, and there's a cacophony of sound coming from the twittering birds warning the forest's inhabitants of your arrival. It is not long before you come to a fork in the path. 'We need to go left,' Hakasan says firmly. 'Yaztromo lives west of here.' Turn to **252**.

239

The market square is soon a place of frantic hustle and bustle as traders haul their goods into the square, with everybody trying to be first to set up their stalls. Early customers arrive dressed in fancy headgear and long, colourful robes, darting between the stalls, scouring the tables looking for bargains. The place is awash with noise, with traders and entertainers shouting loudly to attract custom. There are arm wrestlers, fortune tellers, magicians, snake charmers, and even an organ grinder with his pet monkey collecting coins in a tin mug from onlookers. A shifty-looking girl, perhaps eighteen or nineteen years old, with long black hair and wearing a dark grey belted smock and black leggings, momentarily catches your eye as she walks past. She is following an old man who is carrying a small canvas backpack. Suddenly a blade appears in her hand from nowhere, and you watch her deftly slice open the bottom of the man's backpack. She slips her hand inside and takes out a leather pouch, turning quickly to disappear into the crowd. If you want to challenge the thief, turn to **387**. If you want to ignore the robbery and look around the market, turn to **247**.

240

The owner of the timber yard leaves after a few minutes, and you are left alone with Olaff the Ogre. You ask him some questions but he doesn't reply. You give up trying to talk to him, and carry on piling beams on to the shelves. The owner comes back an hour and a half later, by which time you have finished loading the shelves and are quite exhausted. Lose 1 *STAMINA* point. He walks up to you and says with a smirk on his face, 'Well done, you can go now.' You ask him for payment and he looks at you quizzically and says, 'Payment? What payment?' The Ogre sidles up alongside him, grinning, brandishing an oak club. If you want to fight the Ogre, turn to **113**. If you would rather go back to the market square to walk down Beggar's Alley, turn to **283**.

You scan the many rows of bookshelves and pull out a large leather tome entitled *Demon Princes*. You flick through the pages and open the book at the chapter headed 'Skeleton Demons', where you find a page dedicated to Zanbar Bone. You read that he was born in Fang, the son of two merchants who were secret cultists devoted to the Demon Princes of Titan. Bone went on to study magic in the Forest of Yore and later developed a bitter rivalry with Yaztromo and Nicodemus. He hated them both, and turned evil to learn dark magic to defeat them. However, Bone lost a firestorm battle of magic with his former mentor and teacher, the archmage Vermithrax, and was severely wounded and reduced to nothing more than a barely living skeleton. He disappeared into the night and was not seen again for decades. He reappeared as a Skeleton Demon, known as the Night Prince, and ruled parts of northern Allansia from his Black Tower with the help of his undead and demonic followers. His powers are many, including his ability to paralyse and hypnotize victims, or to destroy them with demon fire and magical energy. The most alarming fact about Zanbar Bone is that defeating him is never permanent. He always returns from the Demon Plain more powerful than ever before, and new ways must be found to defeat him. 'So now you know who we are dealing with,' Yaztromo says solemnly, looking over your shoulder. 'We need Nicodemus's help. You must go to Port Blacksand tomorrow. You'll find him in his wooden hut beneath Singing Bridge. He won't want to come, but you have to bring him here. We need all the help we can get to defeat Zanbar Bone when he reappears. Anyway, that's tomorrow's task. For now, let's eat and enjoy each other's company.' Turn to **14**.

242

You see an old tree trunk with crumbling bark which is host to a cluster of fiery-red capped mushrooms. Your stomach rumbles noisily and you realize just how hungry you are after your exploits in Skull Crag. If you want to eat some of the mushrooms, turn to **285**. If you would rather look for something else to eat, turn to **224**.

243

You are sprayed with acidic sap, which eats into your flesh. Lose 4 *STAMINA* points. If you are still alive, you watch it continue to pump out of the creeper, causing a foul-smelling cloud of vapour to rise from the ground, hissing like gas. It makes you cough, and you have no choice but to follow Nicodemus into the tower, where Hakasan slams the door shut behind you. Turn to **279**.

244

You find a folded piece of paper jammed into the crack in the wall. You pull it out and go back up the steps to read what is written on it. It's a grim message which must have been written by the person who turned into the zombie you encountered in the cellar. It tells of his terrifying experience of being bitten by a zombie whilst mining for gold in Moonstone Hills. The other miners, fearing he might bite them, brought him to the ruined cottage and locked him in the cellar, leaving him to rot. It ends with an apology, saying, 'If I attacked you, I am sorry. It was not of my own doing but of the zombie I will have become. All that is mine is now yours. Look under the steps.' If you want to go back down into the cellar to look under the steps, turn to **391**. If you would rather leave the cottage to carry on towards Moonstone Hills, turn to **164**.

245

Another arrow finds its mark, and you reel back from the impact of it hitting you in the shoulder. Lose 2 *STAMINA* points and 1 *SKILL* point. Hakasan helps you pull the arrow out of your shoulder and stop the bleeding. Turn to **372**.

246

The sunlight is fading fast, and long shadows creep across the forest floor, making everything look eerie, but you take comfort knowing you can't be too far away from Yaztromo's Tower. Turn to **333**.

247

There are plenty of things in the market that you would like to buy, especially the food, but you are penniless. You see a slim, bald-headed man with a long face and unusually long ears who is wearing a black waistcoat over a white shirt tucked into tight-fitting black trousers. He is sitting on a spindle-back chair at a small, green baize-covered table on which three playing cards are lying face down. He stares at you with a piercing look and asks, 'How much is that sword of yours worth to you? Would you dare to play a little game of Find the Lady? If you win, I'll give you 5 Gold Pieces. If you lose, you will give me your sword in exchange for mine. What could be fairer than that?' If you want to play his game, turn to **291**. If you would rather leave the market square, turn to **58**.

248

The vial lands intact on a patch of grass some twenty metres away. Hakasan looks at you in a state of shock and says, 'We are very lucky the vial didn't break. It could have been the end of us. But let's not worry about that now.' Turn to **321**.

249

You shake your head and tell the man that you are not from Port Blacksand. 'Neither am I,' he continues. 'My name is Mungo. I sailed here yesterday from Oyster

Bay with a cargo of fish which I sold this morning in the market for a tidy profit. I spent it all on anchors, rope and fishing nets to sell in Oyster Bay. I've had a good day's business, I can tell you. I'm sailing back this afternoon, leaving on the next high tide. I'm not sure what brought you here, but if you have got nothing planned, I'm looking to hire a crew if you are interested? My deckhand has gone missing.' If you want to agree to sign on as a deckhand, turn to **129**. If you want to decline Mungo's job offer, you can either join the men playing their dice game (turn to **16**) or leave the tavern to walk down Harbour Street towards Singing Bridge (turn to **63**).

250

It doesn't take long to gather enough branches to build a bivouac. You start by making a tripod using the three longest branches, which you tie together at one end with a long strip of thin bark. You lean the remaining branches against the tripod until the bivouac is complete, leaving a small opening at the bottom to climb through. Happy with your shelter, you rummage through your backpack and find a few scraps of food to eat. Add 1 *STAMINA* point. It's a cool evening but you should be warm enough under your blanket inside the bivouac. If you want to build a campfire nevertheless, turn to **144**. If you would rather go straight to sleep, turn to **107**.

Lurching towards you is a Sporeball

251

You continue hacking your way through the thick bushes and undergrowth of the dense forest. You come to a tree stump which has been carved into the shape of an ancient throne, above which there is a dented pewter mug hanging in mid-air on a piece of string tied to a high branch of a nearby tree. A note written on a piece of paper inside the mug says, *Welcome to the Throne of Wishes. You may make one wish at a cost of 1 Gold Piece. Drop a coin into the mug, sit down on the throne and make your wish.* If you want to pay 1 Gold Piece to make a wish, turn to **112**. If you would rather keep on walking, turn to **348**.

252

The narrow path twists and turns through the dense forest before petering out into thick undergrowth, and you have to use your sword to cut a way through. Progress is slow, but you press on. You come to a small clearing where thousands of flying insects are hovering in the sunlight. There is a very bad smell in the air which is coming from the rotting carcass of a deer in the centre of the clearing. There is a cluster of round sponge-like fungi growing out of the carcass, deep red in colour, each the size of a large pumpkin. When you walk into the clearing, a fungus slides off the carcass and short-hops over to you on its squat, concertina-like legs. It is covered with holes which open each time it lands on the ground, puffing out clouds of red dust into the air. Lurching towards you is a SPOREBALL, a giant parasitic fungus which is contaminating the air with a cloud of toxic dust containing millions of poisonous micro-spores. Will you:

Attack the Sporeball with your sword?	Turn to **34**
Pour fireroot juice on the Sporeball?	Turn to **105**
Hold your breath and run through the clearing?	Turn to **232**

253

The Norgul accepts your offer, and you hand over the jar of eyeballs. It smiles with fake gratitude before smashing you in the face with the jar. Lose 2 *STAMINA* points. You reel back from the blow and draw your sword. Turn to **90**.

254

Bignose breathes in deeply through his huge nostrils and says, 'Rumour has it there is a dungeon somewhere deep beneath the forest where the Eye of the Dragon can be found. To find the entrance, all you need to do is find the woodcutter's hut, and that's like finding a needle in a haystack! If I were you, I'd try your luck in Firetop Mountain. They say the place is filled with gold. Or there's always Baron Sukhumvit's Deathtrap Dungeon in Fang. Lots of gold to be won there if you manage to come out alive. Nobody ever has, mind you. Right, I must be on my way. I've got my second cousin to find. Cheerio!' The Dwarf walks past you, whistling happily to himself, and is soon out of sight. Turn to **246**.

255

You climb aboard the cart and sit next to the driver, who introduces himself as Egbert. It's a slow and bumpy ride over cobblestones as the cart wends through the narrow streets of Chalice to the main gates. You give Egbert 1 Copper Piece, which he thanks you for, saying, 'A few words of advice for you. There's somebody from Chalice who makes funny wooden boxes which he hides in caves and the like. If you find one, be careful when you open it. That's all I'm saying. Good luck on your adventure, stranger. You'll need it!' You thank Egbert for the ride, jump down from the cart, and walk out through the gates, waving goodbye to him. Turn to **64**.

256

Bignose is delighted with the trade, and thanks you over and over again. He slaps you on the back, and tells you that he must be on his way. 'I need to find my second cousin before I go back to Stonebridge with the Rune Ring, so I'll say goodbye now. Cheerio!' The Dwarf walks past you, whistling a happy tune, and is soon out of sight. On closer inspection, you see the pendant has a maker's mark on the back, the initials *JF*. 'It must have been crafted by Jadan Fam,' Hakasan says excitedly. 'His dragonfly pendants are worth a fortune!' If you want to wear the pendant around your neck, turn to **135**. If you would rather put it in your pocket, turn to **218**.

257

You place your arm through the leather straps on the back of the shield and rattle your sword against the bronze face. It makes a loud clatter which echoes down the valley. Hakasan salutes you, calling out to congratulate you on finding a Dwarf warrior shield. Add 1 *SKILL* point. Delighted with your new piece of armour, you walk on. Turn to **359**.

258

You make sure Hakasan is comfortable before setting off. It doesn't take you too long to return to the tree house. You climb up the ladder and look around the room. You see that there is a drawer in the table which you hadn't noticed earlier, and pull it open to find a small wooden box with a plain lid. You shake the box and hear something rattling inside. If you want to open the box, turn to **161**. If you would rather leave it in the drawer and look for something else, turn to **189**.

259

You pull hard on your reins, bringing Stormheart to a halt, whinnying loudly in protest. You dismount quickly and climb on to the plinth, knife in hand, to free the captive woman. But it's a trap! The woman throws back her hood, and you see her midnight-black face, pointed ears and an evil glint in her bright green eyes. You have been ambushed by a DARK ELF who is armed with two long serrated knives! Two female Dark Elf accomplices jump out from behind the plinth to join her in the attack. You must fight the Dark Elves one at a time.

	SKILL	STAMINA
First DARK ELF	8	6
Second DARK ELF	8	7
Third DARK ELF	7	7

If you win, turn to **227**. You may *Escape* at any time during the fight by whistling for Stormheart to come alongside and jumping into the saddle. You throw your knife at the Elf closest to you, and urge Stormheart on towards Port Blacksand. Turn to **66**.

260

The horse and cart is soon far away, and you decide to follow its tracks to Catfish River. Ahead you see a brown sack on the ground which must have fallen off the cart. You untie it to find it is filled with carrots, and eat them until you are full. Add 2 *STAMINA* points. You carry on following the cart tracks, scanning the horizon for the elusive Chaos Warrior, but don't see anybody who looks remotely like him. You keep thinking about Hakasan, who you left injured and alone in Darkwood Forest, and hope she is safe. The cart tracks finally lead you to Largo, a small village on the banks of Catfish River west of Darkwood Forest. The villagers are friendly river folk, who spend their days ferrying people and goods up and down Catfish River on their flat-bottomed boats. You walk round the village asking everybody you meet if they have seen a Chaos Warrior in the vicinity. The replies are all negative until one very tall and stocky man by the name of Onx tells you that his cousin was paid 5 Gold Pieces to take a Chaos Warrior to Port Blacksand earlier in the day. 'My cousin was too frightened to say no. I can ferry you to Port Blacksand for 2 Gold Pieces if you wish?' the boatman says in a friendly voice. If you want to accept his offer, turn to **303**. If you would rather decline his offer and head back to help Hakasan, turn to **9**.

261

One of the men drops his club, and it falls on to the cobblestones with a loud clatter. You spin round just in time to see three ROBBERS who are about to jump on you. You must fight them one at a time.

	SKILL	STAMINA
First ROBBER	6	6
Second ROBBER	6	5
Third ROBBER	7	6

If you win, turn to **163**. You may *Escape* at any time during the fight by throwing 3 Gold Pieces up in the air for the robbers to fight over and running off down Thread Street. You turn sharp left down a narrow alleyway, and then turn right at the end into Palace Street. Turn to **371**.

262

The man smiles, turning over the card to reveal a jack of spades. 'Hard luck, stranger,' he says hollowly. 'I'm afraid you failed to find the lady. Your sword, please.' If you want to hand over your sword, turn to **4**. If you want to ask him to turn over the queen of spades card before handing over your sword, turn to **155**.

263

The thundering noise of galloping hooves gets louder as the horseman approaches. You see that the rider is wearing flowing black robes which trail behind him in the wind. You raise your arm to stop the horseman, but he carries on at full speed, blowing his hunting horn and gesturing at you to get out of the way. The horse bears down on you, and you have to dive out of the way to avoid being hit. *Test Your Luck*. If you are Lucky, turn to **100**. If you are Unlucky, turn to **361**.

264

You ride along a dusty track towards the main city gates, where there are gruesome reminders on display to serve as a warning to all who enter Port Blacksand – skulls on wooden spikes and starving criminals locked inside iron cages suspended from the city wall. As you approach the main gate, you need no reminding of the danger that awaits you inside the city, which is run with an iron fist by Lord Azzur and his Imperial Guards, who bleed payment from all who live there. It is known as the City of Thieves for good reason, being the preferred port of call for every pirate and freebooter of the Western Ocean, and home to Allansia's most notorious thugs and robbers. You draw your steed to a halt at the main gate, where you are met by a guard wearing a black chain-mail vest under his black cloak, and an iron helmet which virtually covers his face. 'What brings you to Port Blacksand?' he asks aggressively. Before you have time to answer, he says, 'Your horse is a fine steed. You must be very wealthy. Lord Azzur commands an entry fee of 10 Gold Pieces from people of your stature.' If you want to pay 10 Gold Pieces to enter Port Blacksand, turn to **207**. If you don't have 10 Gold Pieces or do not want to pay that amount, you will have to ride back to Flax to find Cris and hire a rowing boat. Turn to **41**.

A shrivelled, hunched-over old hag

265

You step warily into the gloomy cave and notice small footprints on the sandy floor. Without warning, a soul-chilling howl breaks the silence. From out of the shadows at the back of the cave steps a shrivelled, hunched-over old hag with long, thick grey hair and ragged clothes. The skin on her face is dry and wrinkled, and her eyes are sunken in their sockets and jet black in colour. Her thin, loose-skinned arms and scrawny hands with blackened nails are stretched out in front of her. When she opens her mouth to scream again, you see she has no teeth at all. The wretched creature is a PLAGUE WITCH and you must fight her.

PLAGUE WITCH   *SKILL 5*   *STAMINA 5*

If you lose any Attack Rounds during combat, the Plague Witch will have touched your skin and infected you with worm plague, which will quickly turn your eyes black and make you go blind, just like her. It will be impossible for you to continue your quest. Your adventure is over. If you win without losing any Attack Rounds, turn to **375**.

266

The apples are crisp and juicy, and the cheese is crumbly and very tasty. Add 2 *STAMINA* points. If you have not done so already, you can either try on the signet ring (turn to **141**) or drink the purple liquid (turn to **127**). If you would rather leave the other items and continue your journey to Yaztromo's Tower, turn to **383**.

267

With your heart pounding in your chest, you watch in amazement as Zanbar Bone's skull shatters on impact into tiny pieces. The Demon's skeletal body teeters for a second, and topples over sideways. Every Skeleton left standing immediately drops to the ground in a crumpled heap of bones. You step through the pile of bones to where Zanbar Bone's headless body is lying. One of his skeletal arms rises up slowly, with his index finger pointed at you. Hakasan walks over and chops off the hand, and everybody looks on in horror as his bones turn to dust that is blown away by a sudden gust of wind. 'I don't think we have seen the last of Zanbar Bone,' Nicodemus says quietly. 'Let's not worry about that now,' Yaztromo says reassuringly, putting his arm around the shoulders of his old friend. 'For now Allansia is safe. Let's go inside and celebrate.' Turn to **400**.

268

After you hand over the bag of nails, the man opens his shoulder bag to produce a large cob of brown bread and a small stoppered pot. He tears off a big chunk of bread, uncorks the pot, and pours a generous slug of thick honey all over the bread, some of it trickling on to his fingers as he hands the bread to you. You take it from him and wolf it down. Add 1 *STAMINA* point. Leaning on his broom, the man licks his sticky fingers noisily and says, 'I've got snake oil if you want it. It's the real stuff, you understand? No snake bite will harm you if you rub this druid's lotion on it. I need twine. You got any?' If you want to trade your twine for a small bottle of snake oil, turn to **365**. If you would rather politely refuse his offer and leave the market square, turn to **58**.

269

The bearded man appears very pleased that you want to play a game of Dungles and Draggles with him. He picks up his dice, shakes them manically, kisses his hands for luck, and rolls the dice across the table. 'A 5 and a 2. Perfect! Seven will give you something to think about,' he announces happily. 'Are you going to roll higher or lower?' he asks, handing you his dice to roll. If you possess Lucky Bones and want to use them instead of his dice, they will increase your roll by 4. If you think the total will be higher than 7, turn to **101**. If you think the total will be 7 or lower, turn to **237**.

A sharp pain shoots up your arm the moment you put your hand inside the gauntlet. You try to take it off, but are unable to do so. You are wearing a cursed Gauntlet of Ruin. Lose 2 *SKILL* points and 2 *LUCK* points. You feel incredibly dizzy, and barely able to walk. You stagger off the path, slump down in the undergrowth and fall fast asleep. You wake up hours later with somebody tapping you on your shoulder. You sit up with a start, and recognize the familiar face of Hakasan kneeling over you, grinning. 'Having a nice nap?' Hakasan asks mischievously. Suddenly her expression changes, and she says in a serious voice, 'We can't just ignore what happened back there. I couldn't walk away without knowing the truth. You have to come with me to find Yaztromo. We have to warn him. He might be under attack even as we speak.' You agree that her reasoning makes perfect sense, and apologize for thinking otherwise earlier. She asks about the gauntlet and you explain what happened. You take a swig of water from your water bottle whilst Hakasan cuts the gauntlet away from your hand with a small blade. 'That should stop you from losing any more strength. Now we can get on with our quest. Deep down I knew you would come with me,' Hakasan says with a wry smile. 'Come on, we've got to go back the other way. Yaztromo lives west of here.' Turn to **2**.

271

The chamber pot crashes to the ground in front of you, breaking into tiny pieces. The woman curses and slams her bedroom window shut. You peer through the windows of the remaining houses, but there doesn't seem to be anybody at home. You decide to walk over to the shops. Turn to **305**.

272

You walk outside with Hakasan and Yaztromo, and are astonished to see that the limestone blocks are now stained black up to a height of five metres. Yaztromo sighs, and says, 'It's speeding up. You've probably got two days at the most to get back here with Nicodemus before Bone rematerializes.' He walks round to the back of his tower and reappears a few minutes later holding the reins of a magnificent bright-eyed chestnut-brown stallion. 'This is Stormheart. He is my pride and joy. He will carry you to Port Blacksand. Ride like the wind and do not stop for anything or anyone. After leaving Darkwood Forest, head west towards Catfish River, and keep riding all the way to Black's Bridge. It will be the first bridge you come to. Make sure you pay 1 Gold Piece to cross the bridge or Bartholomew Black will be none too happy. Keep heading west along the north bank of the river until you reach Port Blacksand. The guards might give you some trouble, but that's normal.' You thank Yaztromo for his advice and climb into the saddle. Hakasan and Yaztromo wish you luck and wave goodbye, and with a kick of the heel you are off, galloping at full speed through the forest, ducking under branches and jumping over fallen trees. You soon reach the southern edge of the forest, and head west towards Catfish River. You ride past a small village on the south bank, but with Yaztromo's words ringing in your ears, you do not stop. An hour later you see a large wooden plinth ahead on which there is a woman bound with ropes to a wooden post. She is dressed in black leggings and boots with a black hooded cloak concealing her face. All you can see is her long black hair. She has the appearance of Hakasan, but you wonder how she could possibly have got here before you. You hear her anguished cry for help as you get closer, begging you to stop and release her. If you want to stop to rescue the woman, turn to **259**. If you want to ride on past her, turn to **66**.

273

You take the jar of eyeballs out of your backpack, and hold it in front of you as you step into the Norgul's lair. The creature's lower jaw drops down in amazement, and it lets out a ferocious roar which causes drool to trickle out of its open mouth and down its chin. 'A jar of eyeballs!' it says slowly in a deep, rasping voice. 'This must be Uzzuk's lucky day.' The Norgul lumbers towards you, arms outstretched with evil intent. If you want to shout out that you will smash the jar on the ground unless it stops in its tracks, turn to **42**. If you would rather drop the jar and draw your sword to fight the Norgul, turn to **17**.

274

You creep up behind the guard and hit him on the back his head with the hilt of your sword. Hc falls backwards and you catch him in your arms, dragging him down Palace Street into Snake Alley. You put on the man's black chain-mail vest, studded shoulder pads, black cloak and his iron helmet which virtually covers your face. As you pick up his shield, you realize you are being watched by a gang of thieves who followed you into the alleyway. 'You better leave something for us or clse!' their burly, scar-faced leader says threateningly. You tell him they can keep anything they want, pushing past him to walk into the street to go back to Palace Square to wait for the changing of the guard. You don't have to wait long before ten guards march out of the palace grounds to relieve the guards outside. You join the guards returning to the palace, marching along at the back of the line into the palace grounds past two heavily armed Trolls in the Imperial Guard on gate duty. Turn to **86**.

275

A brass bell rings loudly as you push open the heavy door of the jeweller's shop. The Man-Orc glares at you suspiciously, his hand resting on the hilt of the sword on his belt. 'Don't be concerned by Crusha. He won't hurt you unless you do something stupid like try to rob me!' the old man says calmly. 'I see from your attire that you are not from these parts. Would you like to purchase something? Or perhaps you may have some treasure to sell to me?' You look at the glass cabinets as though interested in buying something, but there is nothing on display that you can afford. If you have a gold rabbit charm that you wish to sell, turn to **396**. If you would rather leave the jeweller's and walk to the end of the street, turn to **82**.

276

Although injured, you have faith in your ability to shoot a bow and arrow. The unseen man calls out again, saying, 'Sorry, I lied. But what did you expect? We're the Black-Eyed Bandits. We rob people. Lots of people. We're not going to kill you. We are just going to take everything you have and be on our way. Keep your heads down and don't do anything you might regret.' Six hooded men appear from behind the trees, each of them armed with a bow and arrow. The colour of their clothes is light and dark brown, blending in with the forest. The bandits have long black hair and eye sockets blackened with charcoal dust. If you want to stay hidden behind the tree trunk, turn to **152**. If you want to fire an arrow at each of the Bandits in quick succession, turn to **65**.

277

Getting a contribution towards a new boat calms Onx down. As soon as you are back in Largo, you hand over the Gold Pieces in payment for the bottle of healing potion. Onx apologizes for shouting at you, and gives you some fresh fish to eat and a cup of goat's milk. Add 2 *STAMINA* points. He asks his friends in the village, but there are no more boats to hire to take you to Port Blacksand until tomorrow, so you decide to go back to Darkwood Forest. You are about to leave when Onx asks if you would like to buy a pair of bone dice that are handmade by the elders of the village. He tells you that they will bring you luck in any dice game, and are a bargain at 2 Gold Pieces for the two. If you want to buy the dice, turn to **73**. If you would rather politely refuse, turn to **110**.

278

The campfire is nothing more than a few glowing embers, and no deterrent to the Hippohog. Despite feeling dizzy and barely able to lift your sword, the fight begins. Reduce your *SKILL* by 3 for this battle.

HIPPOHOG   *SKILL* 9   *STAMINA* 8

If you win, turn to **61**.

Returning as a demon prince, he is evil personified

279

You follow Hakasan up the winding staircase to the library, where Yaztromo is pacing anxiously up and down. He smiles on seeing his good friend Nicodemus, and gives him a big bear hug. Hakasan looks out of the window and makes a solemn announcement: 'He's arrived.' You walk over to the window and look out to see Zanbar Bone, scythe in hand, leaning on silk cushions of an ornate gilt throne carried on the shoulders of four black-robed Skeletons wearing crowns. Returning as a Demon Prince, he is evil personified. His unmistakable spiked skull is now twice the size it was before, and he has grown bat-like wings and cloven hooves. The Skeletons' army parts down the middle to allow their leader a passageway to the front. There is a gigantic five-metre-tall tentacled beast following behind the throne, hideous in appearance, the like of which you have never seen before. You hurriedly decide your battle plan with Yaztromo, Nicodemus and Hakasan. You volunteer to lead the attack on Zanbar Bone. Hakasan says she will defend you from the onrushing Skeleton horde. Nicodemus says he will be at your side casting spells. Yaztromo claps his hands, and says, 'And I will stand on your other side casting spells. Good! We have a plan. The Demon Prince will taste our most powerful magic today.' He pours green juice from a stoppered flask into a cup, and tells you to drink it. You immediately feel invigorated. Add 2 *SKILL*

points and 2 *STAMINA* points. You run downstairs to the ground floor and open the door on to a scene of total chaos. Zanbar Bone is standing on his throne, laughing manically. His army of Skeletons are rattling their swords against their shields, a deafening sound of clashing steel which is painful to your ears. Suddenly he raises his arms skywards, and his troops stand to attention, rigid and upright. All is quiet for a few seconds before the silence is broken by the distant sound of buzzing. A dark cloud appears in the sky and the buzzing sound grows louder. The cloud flies down towards you like a large flock of birds. But this is not a flock of birds – it is a plague of insects controlled by Zanbar Bone. If you are wearing a dragonfly pendant, turn to **308**. If you are not wearing this pendant, turn to **183**.

You sit down at the table to wait for the tree house dweller to return home. You don't have to wait long before you hear the sound of rustling leaves below. The rope ladder suddenly creaks under the weight of somebody climbing up it. You motion to Hakasan to be ready to grab whoever appears through the trapdoor, but nobody appears. 'I don't know who you are, but you have no right to be in my house! You are trespassing!' a voice calls out from below. 'Leave now or I will fill the room with poisonous gas and feed you to the wolves.' If you want to shout down to the man to say that you know he is Gurnard Jaggle and want to ask him about the puzzle box you found in Skull Crag, turn to **213**. If you want to keep quiet and wait for him to come up, turn to **133**.

281

You begin your climb of Skull Crag, scrambling up the bare rock face with ease. You reach a ledge twenty metres up, and notice a stack of sun-bleached branches propped up against the rock face. You move the branches to one side to reveal a crack in the rock which is less than a metre wide. The opening is just as described on Murgat Shurr's map. You light your lantern and squeeze through the crack to find yourself in a narrow man-made tunnel which has a low ceiling. The air is cool and still, and has a slight musty smell. You walk along the tunnel for some fifty metres before coming to a junction. If you want to go left, turn to **301**. If you want to go right, turn to **169**.

282

Finbar pockets the Gold Pieces, and spends the next fifteen minutes working busily at his bench fixing, cleaning and polishing your pistol. He hands it back to you with a smile, clearly proud of his work. 'I've put a new flint in the hammer, which should give off a good spark when you fire it, and I've loaded the barrel with flash powder and a lead ball. The rest of the black powder is in this leather pouch, and a spare lead ball in case you need it,' he says, placing the pouch on the counter. 'If I may give you a few words of advice – keep the black powder away from naked flame or you might blow yourself up!' You bid Finbar farewell, and leave his shop to walk to Singing Bridge, with the pistol tucked into your belt. Turn to **118**.

283

Beggar's Alley is a narrow, potholed dirt track, hardly wide enough to drive a horse and cart down. Dark and decrepit stone and wood houses line the alley, all of them long in need of repair. There is rubbish everywhere, and the putrid stench of open sewers fills the air. Beggars in ragged clothing stand hunched in doorways, their arms outstretched like lost souls pleading, hoping that you might gift them a coin or two. If you have any Copper Pieces that you wish to give to the beggars, turn to **74**. If you would rather walk on to the T-junction at the end of the alley, turn to **311**.

284

With the daylight fading, you walk as fast as possible through the forest. Hakasan says that there is a good chance that you will reach Yaztromo's Tower before nightfall. She suddenly stops in her tracks and tells you to stop. 'What's that noise?' she whispers. 'Can you hear that clicking sound?' You nod, and soon find out what is making the chilling noise. The bushes in front of you part, and the head of a GIANT CENTIPEDE appears through them. It is three metres long and is protected by hard, chitinous plates which rub together to make the clicking sound. It has large protruding mandibles and scuttles forward on its many tiny legs to bite you.

GIANT CENTIPEDE   *SKILL 8*   *STAMINA 7*

If you win, turn to **310**.

285

The mushrooms taste a little bitter but do at least fill you up. You set off again, but it is not long before you start to feel unwell. Your stomach is gripped by a sharp pain and you break out in a cold sweat. Moments later you are violently ill. You drop to your knees clutching your stomach, writhing about on the ground in agony. The redhead mushrooms you have eaten are deadly, and you have no suitable antidote. Your adventure is over.

286

You ride like the wind, leaving the plain to enter Darkwood Forest. Stormheart knows his way home, galloping between the trees, twisting and turning through the undergrowth, jumping over tree trunks and streams, and you have to keep your head down to avoid being hit by low branches. Without warning Stormheart comes to a sudden halt, rearing up on to his hind legs, with Nicodemus clinging on to you to save himself from falling off. Ahead you see what has spooked your steed. A vast horde of SKELETONS armed with spears and swords is moving slowly through the forest, their old bones rattling as they march along. They are bumping into each other in the scramble to get to the front of the line of troops. If you want to ride through the Skeletons to reach Yaztromo's Tower, turn to **36**. If you want to ride around the Skeletons, turn to **154**.

287

Your sword misses its target, hitting the stairway instead with a loud splintering sound. As it lunges forward to bite you, you catch sight of the creature in the shaft of daylight shining down from the room above. Its pallid grey skull is covered with festering sores, and its sunken eyes are red-rimmed and lifeless. It has a gaping mouth, the skin torn away on one side to reveal broken black teeth which bite down on your leg. Although the wound is not fatal, the zombie transmits a virus in its saliva which will turn you into a zombie before the end of the day. Your adventure is over.

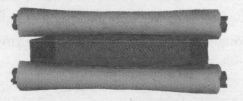

288

As soon as you have finished your breakfast, Yaztromo hands you 15 Gold Pieces and tells you to get ready to depart. You meet him on the ground floor, where he asks you to touch the tips of the fingers of both of your hands with his. A bolt of energy suddenly shoots up your arms and you immediately feel as though the world is on your side and this is going to be your lucky day. Increase your *LUCK* score to 12 points. Turn to **272**.

289

As you walk over to the chest, you see a large globule of green slime drip down from the hole in the ceiling on to the floor with a dull plop, fizzing on contact with the water. A loud squelching sound comes from above, and you look up to see a large gelatinous blob appear in the hole in the ceiling. Turn to **174**.

290

One of the three robbers runs up to you on tiptoes and smashes you over the head with his club, knocking you to the floor. Lose 2 *STAMINA* points. You stagger to your feet, head spinning, trying to focus on your attacker as the robber's two accomplices join in. You must fight them one at a time. Reduce your *SKILL* by 2 points during this fight.

	SKILL	STAMINA
First ROBBER	6	6
Second ROBBER	6	5
Third ROBBER	7	6

If you win, turn to **163**. You may *Escape* at any time during the fight by throwing 3 Gold Pieces up into the air for the robbers to fight over and running off down Thread Street. You turn sharp left down a narrow alleyway, and then turn right at the end into Palace Street. Turn to **371**.

291

The card player rolls his sleeves up and rubs his hands together, eager to play. He turns over the three cards and shows you the queen of spades nestled between two jacks. Slowly turning them face down again, he explains that you have to watch carefully as he switches the order of the cards around. 'Don't take your eye off the lady,' he says in a sly voice. His fingers slide the cards swiftly around the green baize, switching them back and forth, faster and faster. You concentrate as hard as you can, keeping your eye on the card you think is the queen. Finally he lifts his fingers and claps his hands together. You are virtually certain that the queen is still in the middle. 'Right, stranger, find the lady!' Will you:

Choose the card on your left?	Turn to **40**
Choose the card in the middle?	Turn to **262**
Choose the card on your right?	Turn to **184**

The Norgul stops, sniffs the air and looks around

292

Ahead you see the tunnel leads into a chamber which is lit by oil lamps. As you get nearer you see there is a large iron cauldron suspended above a burning log fire by a chain attached to the ceiling, its simmering contents making dull bubbling and plopping sounds. A huge creature with a large round head lumbers into view with a long wooden spoon in its hand. Dark green in colour, the creature has a bloated torso and stocky arms and legs. Its eyes and ears are small, but it has a wide mouth with bulbous purple lips and long teeth protruding from its lower jaw, many of which are broken. It is wearing a filthy apron which is stained with blood and grime. The NORGUL stops, sniffs the air and looks around, before shuffling over to the cauldron. It dips the wooden spoon into the cauldron and scoops out a spoonful of thick green sludge with an eyeball sticking out. It puts the wooden spoon to its fat lips and noisily slurps down the sludge before sucking the eyeball into its mouth with a loud plop. 'Delicious,' it says in a deep, rasping voice. 'Eyeballs are so succulent. Mmmmmm.' You watch the creature bite down on the eyeball, its jaw slamming shut when the eyeball pops open inside its mouth, whereupon a wide smile of satisfaction spreads across its pockmarked face. To reach the tunnel beyond, you have no choice but to face the Norgul. If you have a jar of sheep's eyeballs that you want to offer to the Norgul to let you pass, turn to **273**. If you would rather run in to attack the creature, turn to **17**.

293

You continue to hack your way through the thick undergrowth, but it is slow and tiring work. Lose 1 *STAMINA* point. If you want to go left, turn to **233**. If you want to go even further right, turn to **355**.

294

You put your ear to the iron door but do not hear any sound coming from the other side. More in hope than expectation, you slide the iron key into the lock. Much to your surprise, the key turns in the lock. It makes a satisfying click, and you pull the door open a fraction to view the corridor beyond. There is nobody around. Wasting no time, you walk as quietly as possible along the corridor to the stairway at the end. There is an old ornamental sword hanging on the wall at the top of the stairwell which you take as your weapon. You make your way quickly to the front door and slip outside unnoticed. You see two guards walking along the perimeter wall and wait until they have gone before heading for the main entrance gates at the end of the gravel path. There are two guards on duty and you have no choice but to walk past them. Trying to act normal, you get within five metres of them before they challenge you. You decide to run for it, and charge past them as fast as you can. One of the guards gives chase but you are able to lose him running through the back streets of Chalice. When you think the coast is clear, you make your way to the main town gates and saunter through, whistling happily to yourself. Turn to **64**.

295

You are confronted by an ugly green-skinned brute of a creature with tiny eyes and tusks protruding from its thick-lipped mouth. Blocking the corridor is a TROLL in black chain-mail armour, another of Lord Azzur's Imperial Guards. The Troll glares at you and says, gruffly, 'What are you doing here?' You can't think of a good answer, and draw your sword to attack the Troll.

IMPERIAL GUARD TROLL   *SKILL 11*   *STAMINA 11*

If you win, turn to **322**.

296

With his clenched fist pointed at the Demon, Nicodemus steps forward and calls on the Ring of Burning Snakes to spit fire. Louder and louder he speaks, using arcane words until a cone of fire shoots out from the mouths of the snakes, enveloping Zanbar Bone in a circle of flame. The Demon throws his head back, laughing manically, the yellow flames merely dancing around his body and causing him no harm. 'White fire! White fire!' Yaztromo screams at Nicodemus, whose pale face is contorted with pain from the effort. Using his supreme mental powers to the full, he shouts even louder, screaming at the top of his voice, which makes the veins on the side of his head pulsate and sweat run down his face. The intensity of heat increases, and the colour of the cone of flame changes from yellow to white, causing the expression in Zanbar Bone's eyes to change from immortal power to extreme fear. 'Now!' screams Yaztromo. 'Now! Bone is trapped in the ring of white flame!' The moment has arrived for you to strike. Will you:

Attack him with your sword?	Turn to **138**
Fire an arrow at him?	Turn to **70**
Fire a flintlock pistol at him?	Turn to **198**

297

The Dwarf's eyes light up at the mention of the name Yaztromo. 'The Grand Wizard is a very good friend of the Dwarfs of Stonebridge. Are you friends of the great man too?' Bignose asks enthusiastically. You reply that whilst you are not a friend of Yaztromo, you need to find him to warn him that he is in grave danger. 'Danger? What kind of danger?' Bignose asks anxiously. You look at Hakasan with your eyebrows raised, and she returns the look and shrugs. If you want to tell Bignose about the imminent return of Zanbar Bone, turn to **165**. If you want to say that you are unable to share your news with him, turn to **329**.

298

The old man's eyes light up. He's clearly very pleased to hear that you are interested in his work. 'That's nice of you to ask,' he says warmly. 'I'm an old man, and most people in Chalice couldn't care less what I do. I make charms. Lucky charms. I've been doing it for thirty-five years. You were kind enough to help so I'm going to give you a gift.' The old man places 4 Copper Pieces in your hand, along with a gold rabbit charm with two tiny rubies for eyes. 'This will bring you good fortune when you need it most.' You thank him, shake his hand, and walk off. If you want to look round the market, turn to **247**. If you would rather leave the market square, turn to **58**.

299

You spin round to see that Hakasan has dispatched her two assailants. A search of the Goblins' belongings yields nothing more than a bag of dried maggots. 'They might be a Goblin delicacy, but I'm not eating them,' Hakasan says with disgust. You suggest that it might be better to go to Darkwood Forest after all. Hakasan agrees. Turn to **139**.

300

You are greeted on entry by a portly man with a round face and a balding head. He is standing behind a small counter in a grey apron and rolled-up shirtsleeves. His slightly downturned mouth makes him look a bit grumpy. His shop floor is crammed with barrels of fireworks, each one labelled with colourful names like wiz-bang and rip-rap and zoom boom. There are some smaller wooden kegs standing on the counter that are marked black powder. 'How can I help you?' the man asks courteously. Will you:

Ask about buying some fireworks?	Turn to **341**
Ask about buying some black powder?	Turn to **39**
Leave the shop and walk to Singing Bridge?	Turn to **118**

301

You head down the narrow left-hand tunnel for twenty metres, the light from your lantern casting eerie shadows on the rough-hewn tunnel wall. You pass by a skeleton lying on the floor. One of its arms is pointed in the direction you are walking, the other is twisted up behind its back. Its upper torso is clad in chain-mail armour. If you want to try on the chain-mail armour, turn to **380**. If you would rather keep walking, turn to **69**.

302

The remaining bandits run forward to attack you, screaming at the top of their voices, their swords raised in the air ready to strike. You must fight the first BANDIT to reach you.

BANDIT   SKILL 6   STAMINA 7

If you win, turn to **50**.

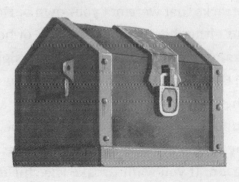

303

You jump on board the flat-bottomed boat and you set off without further delay, with Onx punting effortlessly down river with a long pole. The scenery glides by and you become lost in thought. You are halfway round a bend in the river when Onx suddenly sounds the alarm: 'River Pirates!' A large rowing boat with eight oarsmen on board is headed straight towards you. The captain stands up in the bow, cutlass in hand, shouting orders to his motley crew. Onx tries to steer his boat towards the bank of the river as the pirate boat closes in on you. 'Surrender or die,' the captain shouts. Will you:

Surrender to the River Pirates?   Turn to **339**
Stand and fight the River Pirates?   Turn to **223**
Dive into the river to swim away?   Turn to **151**

304

You zigzag across the valley, heading west, but do not pick up any tracks that were not your own or Hakasan's. 'Gurnard was either here a long time ago, or he covered up his tracks pretty well. I can't find any sign of him being here,' Hakasan shouts over to you. You continue scouring the valley floor for footprints and spot something under a bush which turns out to be a bronze shield left by somebody who must have hidden it there for some reason. If you want to take the shield, turn to

257. If you would rather leave it where it is and walk on, turn to **359**.

305

There are five shops in the street: a florist, a locksmith's, a bookshop, a candle shop and a wool shop. There is a closed sign on the door of the bookshop, and the only other shop of interest to you is the locksmith's. You walk inside and are greeted by a tall, fair-haired man wearing a dark green apron over his striped shirt. He smiles warmly and asks how he can help. You reply that you are about to go on a mission to find a treasure chest hidden in a cave, explaining you might need a special key to open it. 'Well, I can't sell you a key to open a chest I have never seen, so I suggest you make a bulk purchase in the hope that one might do the job. I sell bunches of twenty assorted brass keys for 1 Gold Piece. You might need more than one key, you never know. I've got one bunch of keys left. Do you want to buy it?' Pay the locksmith 1 Gold Piece if you decide to buy twenty brass keys. You chat for a few more minutes before leaving the locksmith's. If you have not done so already, you can try to climb over the wall of the mansion house (turn to **188**). If you would rather make your way through the streets to the main gates to leave Chalice, turn to **64**.

306

On seeing you stand up, the old man throws his glass vial on the floor and disappears quickly down the rope ladder. The vial shatters on impact, releasing a cloud of green gas from out of the broken glass. The gas spirals towards you, enveloping you and making you choke. Gasping for air, you climb down the rope ladder, but cannot escape the encircling cloud of poisonous gas. You drop to your knees, clutching your throat, and fall unconscious. Your adventure is over.

307

It is impossible to open the box by hand. If you want to hack it open with your sword, turn to **186**. If you would rather put the box in your backpack without opening it, turn to **389**.

308

Silver dragonfly pendants made by Jadan Fam were all dipped in the juice of the ground-up Manglewort root, a very rare plant found only in springtime on Icefinger Mountains. The tiniest amount acts as a potent insect repellent. Only Jadan knew where to find the Manglewort, and he never told a soul where they grew to his dying day. Your pendant acts as an invisible shield, keeping the millions of insects at bay until Yaztromo steps in to blast them with a Volcano Spell, which make them all explode, showering the Skeleton horde with insect fragments. Zanbar Bone rages from his throne, and commands his tentacled beast to attack you. Turn to **11**.

309

You tell Nicodemus that you believe Lord Azzur has his gold ring and perhaps you might yet get the chance to take it from him before it's too late. Nicodemus says nothing, and stares ahead at the river. You row on in silence, all the way to the jetty in Flax. You wave to Dod, who is standing nearby, tying up piles of reeds into bundles to carry them home. He walks over to help you tie up the boat, saying, 'Welcome back. I hope you found what you were looking for in that cesspit of a town. Thank you for bringing my boat back. It looks quite a bit bigger than I remember! It's changed colour too.' You apologize and explain what happened, and introduce him to Nicodemus and Luannah. Dod is very happy with his new boat and invites you into his house, where Cris is frying fish. She invites you to stay for supper, and suggests you stay the night too since it's getting late. You accept her offer and wake early in the morning to find Cris and Luannah deep in conversation. Luannah announces that she has decided to stay in Flax to start a new life, and you wish her all the best. Dod brings Stormheart round to the front of the house, and you help Nicodemus mount the horse before climbing on yourself. A light flick of the reins, and Stormheart gallops off at high speed. You look round briefly to see the three of them waving, but you kick on knowing there is no time to lose. Galloping towards Largo, you see a man in a scruffy brown jacket and ragged britches trudging slowly along with the aid of a long walking stick, weighed down by an enormous bulging sack. On hearing the sound of the galloping hooves behind him, he turns around and waves at you with his woollen hat, signalling for you to stop. If you want to stop to talk to him, turn to **93**. If you would rather not waste any time, and ride on to Darkwood Forest, turn to **286**.

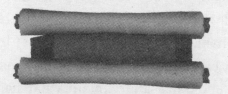

310

You wipe your sword on some leaves to clean off the yellow gunk from the centipede's innards, and tell Hakasan that you have to keep moving or else risk having to sleep out in the forest. But Hakasan complains that her ankle is aching, and asks if she can sit down for a short rest. If you want to agree to stop, turn to **194**. If you want to insist you press on without stopping, turn to **246**.

311

Towards the end of the dark alley, there is a wooden barrel standing in front of the heavy oak front door of a gloomy-looking house built of dark stone with black, shuttered windows bolted shut. Will you:

Look inside the barrel?	Turn to **92**
Knock on the oak door?	Turn to **349**
Walk on to the T-junction ahead?	Turn to **206**

312

Hakasan pushes you down to the ground behind the tree trunk as more arrows fly over your head, fortunately just missing you. You groan loudly as you land on the ground, grimacing from the pain of the arrows which are sticking out of your body. The pain is even more excruciating when Hakasan pulls them out, quickly binding the wounds as best she can. 'Whose idea was it to go to Yaztromo's Tower first?' she teases, trying to cheer you up. But you are in no mood for humour. If you possess a bow and some arrows, turn to **276**. If you do not have a bow and some arrows, turn to **167**.

313

By the time your fight is over, the two guards have disappeared across the bridge, taking Nicodemus with them. Although he's lying in a crumpled heap bleeding profusely, Klash is still breathing. You pull his helmet off his head to take a look at his face. His long black hair is swept back and his eyes are small and completely bloodshot, set back in dark, sunken eye sockets. He has an angry blood-red scar running the length of his face. You remove his gauntlets but are annoyed to see that he is not wearing the Ring of Burning Snakes. You demand to know where the ring is, and where the guards have taken Nicodemus. Klash spits in defiance, and when he speaks, blood trickles from his mouth, making his spiked teeth look even more gruesome. 'I am sorry to disappoint you, but I have given the Ring of Burning Snakes to Lord Azzur for safekeeping,' Klash sneers with contempt. 'As for your wizard friend – you won't find him alive. Lord Azzur will see to that. Nobody will stop the second coming of my master, Zanbar Bone. Allansia is doomed.' Klash laughs in your face before falling silent, defiant to the end. If you want to chase after the guards who kidnapped Nicodemus, turn to **25**. If you want to search the Chaos Warrior's body first, turn to **328**.

314

The dried nettles do nothing to stop the beginnings of paralysis setting in. Lose 1 *SKILL* point and 2 *STAMINA* points. If you want to try snake oil, turn to **128**. If you want to try stikkle wax, turn to **162**. If you do not have either of these items, the paralysis will spread throughout your body and there is nothing you can do to stop it. Your adventure is over.

315

You take your compass out of your pocket and see that you have been heading north-west rather than due west. You turn slightly left and set off again. Turn to **225**.

316

You walk a short distance along the narrow tunnel when you suddenly hear a dull rumbling sound coming from behind you. Turn to **157**.

317

You sit down on a wooden stool at the bar, but the innkeeper grunts and turns his back on you to serve his regular customers. A scrawny, toothless old salt with a straggly beard and ragged clothing sitting on your left chuckles and says, 'Welcome to the Black Lobster!' before he too turns his back on you. Sitting on the stool on your right, a tanned man with a weather-beaten face and a thin, drooping moustache leans towards you and says, 'You're not from around here, are you?' He looks like a pirate with his thin moustache and the gap between his teeth. He is wearing a striped bandana on his head, large earrings and a sleeveless leather waistcoat, and has a long knife tucked into his belt. But his demeanour is friendly enough. If you want to reply to him, turn to **249**. If you would rather ignore him and leave the tavern to head down Harbour Street towards Singing Bridge, turn to **63**.

318

The street sweeper's face lights up with glee when you show him the owl. He bites on it to satisfy himself that it's made of brass. He can hardly contain his excitement and thanks you over and over again. You place the green bottle of oil in your backpack and bid him farewell. He returns to sweeping the square with renewed vigour, whistling even louder than ever. By now, traders and merchants are beginning to arrive in the market square to set up their stalls for the day. If you want to leave the square, turn to **58**. If you would rather stay in the market square for a while longer, turn to **239**.

319

You open the rickety wooden door and walk inside cautiously, sword in hand. Looking at you with surprised expressions on their faces are two MAN-ORCS sitting on stools eating rats with their hands. They have dark green warty skin and are wearing light leather armour. They jump up and grab their short swords, snarling and flashing their spiked teeth and sharp tusks as they leap forward to attack you. Fight them one at a time.

	SKILL	STAMINA
First MAN-ORC	5	6
Second MAN-ORC	5	4

If you win, turn to **229**.

320

Hakasan sees the pendant fall out of your pocket. She picks up it up and hands it back to you, wagging her finger in mock rebuke. You decide it would be better to wear the pendant for safekeeping. Turn to **135**.

321

Hakasan takes the other two items out the box and says, 'I've no idea what the lead ball is for, but you might as well keep it. I'm more interested in what's written on the paper.' You take the paper from her and read out the message on it, which says, *Congratulations, you survived my puzzle box trap. You must be disappointed that the golden amulets were missing from the iron chest. So was I – but I did find a very special treasure! GJ*. Hakasan looks at you in disbelief, and says, 'It looks like Murgat Shurr's map was genuine after all. Gurnard Jaggle must have had a copy of it too. People said he was dead. Is he really still alive? I wonder what he found that made him so happy.' You tell Hakasan that when you were in Chalice, you heard the original owner of the map say that he'd been told there was a gold ring in the chest that was worth more than all the golden amulets put together. It was called the Ring of Burning Snakes and used to belong to a wizard called Nico who would pay a lot to get it back. 'Nico? I've never heard of a wizard called Nico. He must have meant Nicodemus, the grand wizard who lives as a recluse under the Singing Bridge in

Port Blacksand. If this ring was his, why would he be so desperate to get it back? I heard he had given away all his worldly possessions,' Hakasan says, frowning. 'Anyway, I'm going to look for tracks, just in case Gurnard Jaggle was here recently.' If you want to help Hakasan look for tracks, turn to **304**. If you want to look for something to eat first, turn to **117**.

322

A search of the Troll's clothing yields 22 Gold Pieces stolen from prisoners, a silver earring, and a bunch of iron keys hanging on his belt. You grab the items and hurry down the corridor, entering a large chamber which has been converted into a jail. The jail has four cells in it, each with floor-to-ceiling iron bars. The first cell on your left holds four rough-looking ship's crew, all of them with cuts, bruises and black eyes from fighting. The second cell holds two older, unshaven sea dogs in ragged uniforms who look like they have been in jail for years. In the first cell opposite, there is a sad-looking woman in a long dress holding the iron bars and watching your every move, and in the cell next to her is the man you have been looking for, who is sound asleep on his bed, snoring loudly. You take off your helmet and tell the prisoners that you are not a guard, but an adventurer who has come to rescue Nicodemus, pointing to the old man asleep in his cell. 'Why?' the woman asks in a whisper. She has a kind face, and you decide to tell her that you are going to take him to see his old friend Yaztromo. At the mention of the wizard's name, her face lights up. 'Yaztromo?' she says excitedly. 'Is he alive? I feared he might be dead. Has anything happened to his tower? Perhaps I should explain. My name is Luannah Wolff. Months ago the evil tyrant Lord Azzur sent Spirit Stalkers to kidnap me and force my husband, Horace, to help him bring back Zanbar Bone from the Plain of the Undead. Did you know he is going to rule Allansia from Yaztromo's Tower?' Before replying, you unlock her cell door with one of the iron keys and tell her to sit down on the bed. You explain that Yaztromo is alive and well, but that you have some terrible news for her concerning her husband. A look of dread covers her pale face, and she bursts into tears as you relate the tragic tale that led to her husband's untimely death on the day you met him. You leave her to grieve alone whilst you unlock Nicodemus's cell door. The old wizard is still in a deep sleep as a result of being drugged by his kidnappers. 'Set us free and I'll give you some special smelling salts that will wake him up,' the seaman opposite says. You reply, saying you will only unlock his door if he gives you the smelling salts first. He agrees, and passes a small vial to you through the bars. You uncork the vial and place the sharp-smelling salts under Nicodemus's nose. He immediately starts to cough and splutter, and sits bolt upright. He looks at you with a face like thunder. 'Who are you?' he demands. You tell him your story and why you are here to rescue him. Luannah enters his cell and tells you that she wants to come with you to help avenge her husband's death. 'Let us out and we'll come too!' shouts the seaman. 'These are dark days indeed,' Nicodemus says soberly. 'We need to leave immediately. Unlock the cell doors. We'll need all the help we can get to escape from the palace.' You release the six men and make your way back along the corridor and up the stone steps. You push the door open and walk outside. The seamen arm themselves with picks and shovels left behind by the palace gardeners. 'As soon as we see anybody, I'll cast a Time Freeze spell. That will give us one minute to escape through the entrance gates, but not a second longer,' says Nicodemus, who is still a bit unsteady on his feet walking along. Ahead you see some guards milling around the barracks. Two of them spot you and shout the alarm. More guards spill out of the barracks, some armed with crossbows. Nicodemus stops to raise his arms in the air with the palms of his hands pointing towards the oncoming guards. He murmurs arcane words which you do not understand, and suddenly the guards stop moving, standing mid-step as though frozen in time. 'Hurry!' shouts Nicodemus, half shuffling, half walking as fast as he is able. You pass through the entrance gates with seconds to spare, deciding which way to go. 'Let's head for Herring Wharf and board a ship,' shouts one of the seamen.

They all shout 'Aye!' and run across Palace Square. If you want to follow them, turn to **168**. If you want to turn right towards Palace Bridge, turn to **346**.

323

With your sword drawn, you slowly descend the wooden stairway into the semi-darkness. You are about halfway down the steps when a sickly grey hand reaches out from the shadows and grabs your ankle. An unseen creature goes berserk, wailing loudly as it tries to bite your leg. You swing your sword blindly at your attacker. *Test Your Luck.* If you are Lucky, turn to **199**. If you are Unlucky, turn to **287**.

324

Hakasan comes bounding into view with a beaming smile on her face. 'Not one rabbit but two!' she announces with smug satisfaction, dropping the dead rabbits on the ground in front of you. It's not long before you are feasting on spit-roast rabbit to the point where you feel you are going to burst. Add 3 *STAMINA* points. You stoke the fire before retiring to the pigpen, taking it in turns to sleep whilst the other keeps watch. You hear sporadic grunts and growls outside, but the night passes without incident. You set off early next morning towards Darkwood Forest, convinced that your treasure-hunting fortunes will soon change. Turn to **56**.

325

You retrace your steps, and it isn't long before you are back at the spot where you left Hakasan in the forest, but you are alarmed to discover that Hakasan is not there. You wonder if maybe you are in the wrong place, but are certain the tree you are standing next to is the same one Hakasan was leaning against when you left her. 'You took your time, didn't you?' a familiar voice calls out from above. You look up to see Hakasan staring down at you from a high branch of the tree. You ask her how she managed to climb the tree with a broken ankle, to which she replies, 'I used a rope to climb up. I'm stronger than you think! Did you find anything for my ankle?' She lowers herself down to the ground and sits down. You see that her ankle is very swollen and take the jar and bandage out of your backpack. She asks what it is and you reply that the jar contains a yellow paste that smells of rotten eggs and is supposed to be a 'cure-all'. Hakasan uncorks the jar, sniffs the paste and says, 'That smells disgusting, but what have I got to lose? I might as well rub some of it on my ankle.' As soon as she applies the paste on the damaged ankle, the deep cut starts to heal. 'Look!' exclaims Hakasan. 'This is incredible! My ankle is healing. It's still sore but I think I should be able to walk on it.' You tell her it would be wise to stick to the original plan and go to Yaztromo's to warn him about Zanbar Bone and, with luck, you might still be able to track down Klash tomorrow. You bandage Hakasan's ankle and help her to her feet. You make a crude crutch out of a branch for her to support herself on, and set off west at a slow pace. You take the lead, hacking your way through bushes and the thick undergrowth of a dense part of the forest. You stumble upon a tree stump which has been carved in the shape of an ancient throne. There is a dented pewter mug hanging in mid-air on a piece of string tied to a high branch of a nearby tree. A note written on a piece of paper inside the mug says, *Welcome to the Throne of Wishes. You may make one wish at a cost of 1 Gold Piece. Drop a coin into the mug, sit down on the throne, and make your wish*. If you want to pay 1 Gold Piece to make a wish, turn to **112**. If you would rather keep on walking, turn to **348**.

326

The man eyes you suspiciously, wondering why you stopped him. 'I've got nothing worth robbing me for if that's what you're thinking,' he says in a tired voice. You reply that you are about to set off on a treasure hunt in Moonstone Hills and are just trying to collect some provisions before leaving Chalice. 'I wouldn't bother with Barrel Street, trust me,' he says with a knowing look. 'For a Copper Piece, I'll take you to the main gates if you are ready to go now?' Will you:

Pay for a ride to the main gates?	Turn to **255**
Walk back to the market square to go to Armoury Lane?	Turn to **8**
Walk back to the market square to go to Beggar's Alley?	Turn to **283**

327

The howling gale builds into a violent storm. The *Blue Marlin* struggles to climb each mountainous wave before surfing down the other side and crashing into the waiting trough. It is difficult to make good headway under sail, even with Mungo fighting with the tiller to keep his boat on course. You frantically bail water out of the boat with a bucket, but it is exhausting work and drains your strength. Lose 2 *STAMINA* points. At one point a huge rogue wave crashes down on to the decks, almost knocking you off your feet, but you manage to grab the rigging to save yourself. The storm dies down as you come into port, and you both agree you have done enough sailing for one day. Mungo is distraught that his cargo has been washed overboard, and tells you that your services are no longer required. He pays you 1 Gold Piece despite his loss, and you thank him for his generosity. You shake his hand and leave him to repair his boat, and head down Harbour Street towards Singing Bridge. Turn to **63**.

328

You take the Chaos Warrior's gauntlets, which fit you perfectly. Add 1 *SKILL* point. You find nothing in his pockets, but the leather pouch on his belt contains a yellow handkerchief. You unfold it and cannot believe your eyes. Klash lied to you. Lying in the palm of your hand is a large gold ring, an elaborate design of intertwining snakes with their heads locked together, mouths open. It is the Ring of Burning Snakes, the one thing that Nicodemus needs to defeat the Demon Prince, Zanbar Bone. Time is short. You must rescue Nicodemus before Lord Azzur silences him for ever, and return his fabled ring to him. You put the ring in your pocket and run across Singing Bridge in pursuit of the guards. Turn to **25**.

329

Bignose looks at you with a hurt expression on his face, and says, 'Well, if you can't tell me, you can't tell anybody. But never mind because I think you are making all of this up. I'm sorry, but I've got better things to do than stand here listening to your tall tales. I need to find my second cousin, so I'll be on my way. Cheerio!' The Dwarf barges past you, whistling loudly, and is soon out of sight. Turn to **246**.

330

The glass jars are labelled *Dried Deelia Petals*, *Zanhoke Seeds*, *Noop Powder*, *Redthorn Leaf*, *Siff-Saff Paste*, *Lotus*

Flower and *Fireroot Juice.* You can fit three jars in your backpack. If you wish to take any, make a note of which three you take. Finding nothing else of interest, you leave the cabin to carry on to Moonstone Hills. Turn to **134**.

331

Many of the books have tattered covers and missing pages. They are written on a variety of topics such as cabin building, animal traps and growing vegetables, but the one that really catches your eye is an old tome entitled *Crafting Puzzle Boxes* which has an illustration of a stag beetle on the cover. The book is handwritten, each written page filled with detailed ink drawings on how to make intricate boxes with secret compartments, sliding parts and hidden catches. 'Could this be Gurnard Jaggle's home?' Hakasan asks excitedly. You decide to look inside his wooden chest to find out. Turn to **376**.

332

The venom from a Yellowback is quick-acting, and paralysis of your central nervous system soon sets in. Your temperature rises and your heart starts pounding in your chest. Hakasan runs over to help, frantically trying to bleed the poison from the wound, but there is nothing she can do to save you. It's not long before you lose consciousness, never to recover. Your adventure is over.

He is wise-looking and you don't feel threatened despite his cold stare

333

You push on through the forest, spurred on by the fact that you are nearing your destination. The trees thin out a little as you approach the southern edge of the forest, and suddenly you see the top of a huge stone tower poking out just above the treetops ahead. Hakasan whoops for joy, saying, 'Yaztromo's Tower! We've found it!' You walk on as quickly as possible in the fading light, soon arriving at a clearing where the tall tower stands proudly, causing a formidable shadow to be cast across the forest floor. Built with the help of the Dwarfs of Stonebridge, it has been home to the grand wizard Yaztromo for as long as anyone can remember. As you walk towards the great oak door, you are alarmed to see that the limestone blocks at ground level have turned jet black to a height of three metres. Just as you are about to ring the brass bell hanging in the doorway, the door flies open. A ruddy-faced old man with long white hair and a long white beard stands blocking the doorway, staring at you with a deep frown on his face. He is holding a wooden staff and is dressed in long, flowing scarlet robes. His is wise-looking, and you don't feel threatened despite his cold stare. 'Hello. Do I know you? Have we met before? Have you come here to deliver my cakes? If not, you can turn around and be on your way!' he says abruptly. You reply, saying that you have bad news regarding his tower. 'My tower? As if I don't know about my tower! Look at it! It's turning black! It's as though black ink is coming out of the ground and creeping up the walls to stain the beautiful limestone. At this rate it will be totally black before the end of the week! Even my powerful magic can't seem to stop it. It's terrible! Have you any idea what is going on?' You tell Yaztromo that the reason why you have come to see him is to tell him about Zanbar Bone's plans to take over his tower. 'Zanbar Bone! He's coming back, is he? I should have known. If that piece of skeletal detritus thinks he is going to take over my tower and rule Allansia, he's got another think coming! You better come in and tell me all about it.' You enter his tower and follow the grand wizard slowly up his winding wooden staircase. He huffs and puffs his way all the way up to his library on the fourth floor where he slumps down into his favourite armchair, mopping his brow with a bright orange handkerchief. You sit down next him and recount the alarming tale told to you by poor Horace Wolff. 'I see. This is very bad news indeed,' he says, looking glum. 'It's getting late, so I suggest you spend the night here. We'll have some supper and come up with a plan! How hungry are you? Do you want to eat right away? Or would you like to look at my fine collection of books?' If you want to eat immediately, turn to **14**. If you would rather look at Yaztromo's books first, turn to **241**.

334

You walk up to the man and introduce yourself. He looks you up and down, and says dismissively, 'You look like you need a job. I'll pay you 2 Gold Pieces to help Olaff load these shelves. It shouldn't take you more than two hours.' If you want to accept the job offer, turn to **240**. If you would rather go back to the market square to walk down Beggar's Alley, turn to **283**.

335

You begrudgingly hand over a Gold Piece to the old man, who bites on it to make sure it is genuine. Satisfied it is real, he steps aside to let you climb down the rope ladder, and you are soon on your way again to Yaztromo's Tower. Turn to **251**.

336

Your sword will only do minimal damage to the gelatinous flesh of the Lavaworm, which heals almost instantly. Each time you win an Attack Round, the Giant Lavaworm only loses 1 *STAMINA* point instead of 2.

GIANT LAVAWORM   *SKILL 9*   *STAMINA 9*

If you win, turn to **382**.

337

The monstrous creature lumbers forward, its long tentacles curling in and out of its cavernous mouth, trying to snare you. Its iron-like hide is difficult to pierce with normal weapons, but your Venom Sword was crafted with Demon-slayer magic. Add 3 *SKILL* points.

QUAG-SHUGGUTH   *SKILL 12*   *STAMINA 13*

If you win, turn to **362**.

338

Despite its size, the Troll is quick to react. It grabs your leg as you try to kick it, and pulls you through the doorway. With one swipe of its giant hand, it sends you flying down the stone steps to land heavily on the corridor floor below. Lose 1 *SKILL* point and 3 *STAMINA* points. The Troll goes berserk and rushes down the steps to attack you. You stand up and run down the gloomy corridor, turning left at the first junction, trying to escape the angry creature. But a twisted ankle slows you down and you have no choice but to turn and fight the IMPERIAL GUARD TROLL who is closing in on you. You will automatically lose the first Attack Round due to your injury.

IMPERIAL GUARD TROLL   *SKILL 11*   *STAMINA 11*

If you win, turn to **322**.

339

The pirate boat comes alongside your boat with the crew reaching out to take hold of it. The pirate captain orders you both to climb on board his boat, and tells his men to take all of your possessions, including your sword. They chain you by your ankle to a seat in the boat and give you an oar. 'Welcome aboard,' says the sneering captain. 'You are now officially under the command of Captain Crow. Row hard and you might get fed.' You try to convince the captain about the return of Zanbar Bone, but he tells you to stop making up fanciful stories and concentrate on rowing. Wondering about the fate of poor Hakasan, you begin your new life as a river pirate. Your adventure is over.

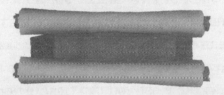

340

You bid farewell to the tracker, walking past her to exit the cave. You step outside on to the ledge where the bright sunlight hurts your eyes, making you squint. You scramble down the crag to the main entrance to the cave. Peering inside, you see nothing but darkness beyond the sunlit entrance. If you want to enter the cave, turn to **79**. If you would rather head west towards Darkwood Forest, turn to **242**.

341

'Certainly! You've come to the right place. I've got the best fireworks in town,' he says with a smile, his tone even more jovial now that you have expressed interest in buying some of his goods. 'My fireworks are made with the finest black powder in Allansia. I buy it from the Lizard Men of Fire Island. So, how many do you want to buy? They cost 1 Gold Piece each. You won't be disappointed when they light up the sky.' You may buy as many fireworks as you wish up to a maximum of ten, which is the most you can fit into your backpack. With the transaction completed, Finbar asks you if you own a flintlock pistol, saying, 'If you do, you should buy some of my black powder to fire it with. I sell a lot of it to pirates and freebooters, and they know good black powder when they see it! It's only 2 Gold Pieces for a pouch of the best.' If you own a flintlock pistol and want to buy some black powder, turn to **39**. If you would rather leave the shop and walk to Singing Bridge, turn to **118**.

342

Hakasan looks deep in thought as you head west, ambling through the tall grasses of the plain without the usual spring in her step. Without warning, four small, sinewy creatures with brown, scaly skin jump up from where they were hiding in the long grass. They are GOBLINS and you must fight them. You take on two of them, which you fight at the same time. During each Attack Round, the Goblins have two attacks.

	SKILL	STAMINA
First GOBLIN	5	5
Second GOBLIN	5	4

If you win, turn to **299**.

343

The baying crowd closes in on you, grabbing your arms. There are too many of them for you to fight. 'Put the thief in the stocks for the rest of the morning. Let it be a lesson and a warning to one and all that crime doesn't pay,' a large, bearded man with braces holding up his baggy britches says in a commanding voice. 'Have your rotten eggs and tomatoes at the ready!' Still protesting your innocence, you are dragged kicking and cursing to the wooden stocks set on top of a stone plinth in the middle of the square. With your wrists and neck firmly

locked in the jaws of the stocks, a loud cheer erupts as the first egg splatters into your face, quickly followed by two more. The barrage continues all morning, some of the more unkind folk hurling potatoes which thump painfully into your face, giving you two black eyes. Lose 1 *STAMINA* point. You are finally released from the stocks at noon in considerable discomfort and decide you should waste no more time in the market square. Turn to **58**.

344

Bignose pauses to look at his treasured weapon for a second before saying, 'Done! I'm not going to argue with anybody who is going to help Yaztromo. The battleaxe is yours!' You thank Bignose for his generosity, and give him the bell and the candle in exchange. He smiles, saying, 'Right, I must be on my way. I've got my second cousin to find. Cheerio!' The Dwarf walks past you, whistling happily to himself, and is soon out of sight. Turn to **246**.

345

The gully opens out on to a rock-strewn valley, at the end of which one hill stands out against all others. Its shape roughly resembles that of a giant human skull, almost as though somebody long ago had carved it that way. It is almost devoid of vegetation and has a rounded top.

Two recesses high up resemble eye sockets, and a large rock sticking out below could pass for a nose. There is an entrance to a cave at ground level which could easily be mistaken for an open mouth. You hurry along the valley as quickly as possible, looking at your map, eager to explore inside Skull Crag. You arrive at the cave and peer inside to see nothing but darkness beyond the sunlit entrance. If you want to enter the cave, turn to **79**. If you would rather climb Skull Crag to find another way in, turn to **281**.

346

You are metres away from Palace Bridge when the guards snap out of their paralysed state and pour out through the palace gates to give chase. They first catch sight of the seamen running across the square and take aim at them with their crossbows. You hear cries for help from two of the seamen who are shot in the leg and stumble to the ground. You do not stop to find out what happens to them, and run over the bridge, turning right into Axeman's Street. You see a rowing boat tied to the steps below, and tell Nicodemus and Luannah to jump on board. You untie the boat, grab the oars and push off, rowing as hard as you can upriver to escape under the arch of the city wall. Guards appear on the bridge, with a Troll Imperial Guard shouting the order for the crossbowmen to fire at you. *Test Your Luck*. If you are Lucky, turn to **221**. If you are Unlucky, turn to **106**.

It's not long before you see a speck of daylight at the end of the tunnel. You arrive back at the narrow entrance to Skull Crag and see the shape of a human figure silhouetted against the daylight. With your sword in hand, you call out to challenge the person standing in your way. You hear a young woman's voice calmly say, 'Put your sword away, I'm not looking for a fight. I picked up your footprints in the valley and followed you here. I thought that whoever made the effort to explore Skull Crag must have a good reason to do so. I'm pleased you made it out alive. What brought you here?' If you want to reply that you are an adventurer looking for treasure, turn to **132**. If you would rather let your sword do the talking and step forward to attack the woman, turn to **363**.

348

The further you go, the more the forest's thick vegetation closes in on you. Long vines hang down from ancient trees, and the blanket of leaves above blots out most of what little light remains of the day. Scrambling over gnarled roots and moss-covered rocks, hacking your way through the dense undergrowth, is tiring and makes for slow progress. Lose 1 *STAMINA* point. 'Are you sure we are still heading west? I swear we passed by here before,' Hakasan says, breathing hard, pointing at a large bush with broad, purple-edged leaves. If you possess a brass compass, turn to **315**. If you do not own a compass, turn to **369**.

349

The large door is yanked open by a huge, bald-headed man wearing a dirty vest and grubby trousers. He looks very angry. 'I hate door-to-door vendors,' he screams in your face. Before you can protest your innocence, he smashes you over the head with a chair leg and slams the door. Lose 2 *STAMINA* points. You decide against knocking on the door again and walk to the T-junction at the end of the alley. Turn to **206**.

350

The only bandit left alive takes aim at you with his bow and fires off another arrow before turning around and disappearing into the forest. *Test Your Luck*. If you are Lucky, turn to **83**. If you are Unlucky, turn to **245**.

351

The liquid is thick and creamy, and tastes of mint. A warm glow spreads through your body and you immediately feel invigorated. Onx's potion is genuine. Add 1 *SKILL* point and 3 *STAMINA* points. You hand the bottle to Hakasan, smiling smugly, and tease her for doubting you. She snatches it from you, scowls and gulps down what's left of the potion. Her scowl soon turns to a smile, and she says with glee that her ankle feels suddenly strong and free from pain. Minutes later the swelling is gone, and she is able to stand and put her full weight on the ankle. 'That's incredible! Thank you, thank you, thank you,' she says happily. You suggest that you should stick with the original plan and go to Yaztromo's Tower to warn him about Zanbar Bone. You take the lead, hacking your way through bushes and thick undergrowth of a dense part of the forest. You stumble upon a tree stump which has been carved into the shape of an ancient throne. There is a dented pewter mug hanging in mid-air on a piece of string tied to a high branch of a nearby tree. A note written on a piece of paper inside the mug says, *Welcome to the Throne of Wishes. You may make one wish at a cost of 1 Gold Piece. Drop a coin into the mug, sit down on the throne and make your wish.* If you want to pay 1 Gold Piece to make a wish, turn to **112**. If you would rather keep on walking, turn to **348**.

352

You bound up the steps, sword in hand, to find yourself standing face-to-face with another MAN-ORC. It points at you and starts screaming and shouting in a language you don't understand. It picks up both swords lying on the floor and runs at you, intent on revenge. You must fight the Man-Orc.

MAN-ORC   SKILL 6   STAMINA 6

If you win, turn to **210**.

353

You cross the square and walk boldly towards the palace entrance. There are two huge guards standing in front of the open gates wearing black armour. They have green skin, tusked mouths, and a rather unpleasant bodily odour wafting around them. They are ugly trolls, civilized enough to speak, but in reality merciless brutes hired by Lord Azzur as Imperial Guards to keep unwanted guests out of his palace. 'Halt!' one of them grunts, pointing his spear at you. If you want to ignore him and walk through the entrance gates waving your hand dismissively at the Trolls, turn to **390**. If you would prefer to try bribing the Trolls to let you in, turn to **5**.

354

You see blood seeping from the needle-like punctures in your skin, and you know you will have to act quickly to prevent the onset of paralysis. You search through your backpack to look for an antidote. If you want to try snake oil, turn to **128**. If you want to try stikkle wax, turn to **162**. If you want to try dried nettles, turn to **314**. If you have none of these items, paralysis will soon set in and there is nothing you can do to stop it. Your adventure is over.

355

You continue your slow journey, carving your way through the thick undergrowth. You arrive back at the large plant with the purple-edged leaves, and realize you have gone in a complete circle. Lose 1 *LUCK* point and 1 *STAMINA* point. If you want to head left, turn to **233**. If you want to keep going right, turn to **293**.

356

Holding the dagger in front of you by the tip of its blade, you take careful aim at your ultimate enemy, with Hakasan screaming at you to hurry. You throw your dagger at the Demon, and watch it fly towards its skull. Roll 1 die and add 1 to the number rolled if your current *SKILL* is 10 or higher. If the total is 1–5, turn to **222**. If the number is 6 or 7, turn to **267**.

357

Four member of the press gang jump on you, taking your sword and tying your arms behind your back. You are pushed next to a forlorn-looking young man wearing a baggy white shirt and black britches who is also tied up. 'Right, lads, put these rats below decks on board the *Toucan* and show them the floors they'll be scrubbing and bilges they'll be cleaning for the next month at sea. Nobody is going to miss these nobodies!' You protest loudly, but there is nothing you can do to stop the press gang dragging you on to their pirate ship. Your adventure is over.

Three blue-skinned goblin-like creatures run out, screaming at the top of their lungs

358

As you approach the scarecrow, its head suddenly lifts, and you see it's not a man made of straw, but a live human being – a sinewy old man with a long beard and straggly hair wearing ragged clothing. 'Help! Help!' he shouts desperately on seeing you. At that moment the cabin door flies open and three blue-skinned goblin-like creatures run out, screaming at the top of their lungs. They are no more than a metre tall, and are wearing red cotton jackets, red pointed hats and red canvas shoes. They have large heads with long pointed noses, and their wide mouths house sharp, jagged teeth and bright red tongues. Their sunken, lizard-like green eyes glaring out from under their pointed hats give them a deranged look, made all the worse by the sight of the big forks and long knives they are holding. They cackle manically as they run forward to stab you in the leg. If you want to fight the BLUE IMPS, turn to **226**. If you want to make a run for it, turn to **116**.

359

You reach the end of the valley where you decide to give up on the search for Gurnard Jaggle's tracks to focus on treasure hunting. You head down the gully, mindful of an ambush, but pass through it without incident. By the time you finally reach the western edge of Moonstone Hills, the sun is low on the horizon. As the shadows lengthen, you hurry north-west across the Eastern Plain towards the tumbledown ruin of an old farmhouse, which looks like a good place to camp for the night. In the far distance you see the great wall of trees which marks the edge of Darkwood Forest. If you want to stay in the ruined farmhouse for the night, turn to **228**. If you want to press on to Darkwood Forest, turn to **136**.

360

He slaps his thigh and says, 'Jolly good,' in a booming voice. He stands up and walks over to you with a big beaming smile spread across his face, his hand outstretched to greet you. Whilst shaking your hand vigorously, he says, 'Good day, dear people. My name is Bignose, for obvious reasons, as you can see! I am the second cousin of Bigleg of Stonebridge. Sadly he went missing some months ago, and I have been searching for him ever since. He looks very much like myself only he doesn't have a big nose! You haven't seen him, have you?' You both shake your heads and tell him that you haven't seen his cousin. 'Ah, that's a shame. I know he's somewhere in the forest. He's searching for the war hammer stolen from Gillibran, our king. What brings you to Darkwood Forest?' If you want to reply that you are on your way to Yaztromo's Tower, turn to **297**. If you want to reply that you are treasure hunters, turn to **143**.

361

You hit the ground hard, landing with a thump. You pick yourself up without realizing that four coins fell out of your pocket. Roll four dice. For each even number, lose 1 Gold Piece. For each odd number, lose 1 Copper Piece. You watch the horseman disappear west in a cloud of dust; whoever it is, he's clearly in a hurry. You decide you might as well help yourself to some corn, eating one cob and saving three for later. Add 1 *STAMINA* point. Still wondering who the horseman was, you set off again, leaving the cornfield behind. Looking east, you estimate it will be dark before you reach Skull Crag, and hope you will be able to find somewhere safe to camp down for the night. Looking south, you see a semi-ruined stone cottage with its thatched roof mostly missing. If you want to take a look inside the cottage, turn to **319**. If you would rather press on towards Moonstone Hills, turn to **164**.

362

The death of Quag-Shugguth makes Zanbar Bone go into a frenzy. With maggots pouring from his mouth, he curses your name. Lightning strikes the ground from the darkened sky, and he steps down from his throne to order his Skeletons forward to attack. Yaztromo casts a Warp Spell on the Skeletons to slow them briefly and give you time to advance, whilst Hakasan launches herself at the Skeletons in front of you, swinging her sword back and forth trying to hack a way through to the Demon Prince. The air is putrid with the smell of Skeletons, their bones grinding against each other in the crush to reach you. But you stay calm and ready yourself for the final battle. If Nicodemus is wearing the Ring of Burning Snakes, turn to **296**. If he is not wearing his special ring, turn to **138**.

363

As you stride towards her, you do not see the tripwire that was put in place by the ninja tracker standing at the entrance to the cave. Your left foot catches on the near-invisible wire and you trip over, knocking yourself out as you land heavily on the rock floor. When you wake up you find yourself tightly bound and gagged, and all your possessions gone. There is little hope that you will ever be found alive unless by Cave Trolls, which is not much consolation. Your adventure is over.

364

You are hit in the leg by an arrow. Lose 1 *SKILL* point and 2 *STAMINA* points. Ignoring the pain, you charge towards the bandits before they have time to reload, swinging your sword in the air. Fight them one at a time.

	SKILL	STAMINA
First BANDIT	6	7
Second BANDIT	7	7
Third BANDIT	7	6

If you win, turn to **22**.

365

The street sweeper seems very happy with the trade. You place the brown bottle of oil in your backpack and bid him farewell. He smiles, nods in gratitude, and goes back to sweeping the square, whistling happily to himself. Just as you are about to walk away, he turns to you, raises one eyebrow, and says, 'I've got skunk oil if you want it? It's the real stuff, you understand? It stinks so bad it would make a charging Minotaur turn and flee! It's my wife's birthday tomorrow. I need an ornament. She likes birds. You got any?' If you want to trade your brass owl for a small bottle of skunk oil, turn to **318**. If you would rather politely refuse his offer and leave the square, turn to **58**.

366

The bearded man thumps the table and shakes his head in disbelief, not very amused that he lost the game of Dungles and Draggles. He pulls the old pistol from his belt and slaps it on the table, saying, 'Here, take it. The flintlock is now yours. I'm not sure if it works, mind.' Pleased with your prize, you head back to the bar. Turn to **89**.

367

It is only when you reach the wicker basket that you realize just how big it is. It contains a huge rectangular block of black stone which has been carved on one side with a scene of an advancing army of Skeleton Warriors being urged on by a robed skeleton figure holding a scythe who has spikes jutting out of its skull, and lizard-like eyes. Beneath the stone block lies a man with dark hair; the lower half of his body has been crushed. You cut the vines keeping the lid of the basket shut to try to pull the man out, but you are unable to free him, even with both of you trying to lift the stone. He stares at you without blinking, his eyes wide open in fear, knowing there is nothing you can do to save him. He reaches out, clutches your arm, and in a stuttering voice says, 'He's coming back. He's coming back! You've got to stop him. You've got to stop him!' The poor man screams out in pain as he tries to sit up to take a drink of water from your flask. Hakasan tries to comfort him whilst he breathes in and out sharply, noisily spraying out water through his gritted teeth. He calms down and starts talking rapidly, desperate to tell his tale. 'Listen carefully, stranger. I don't have long. My name is Horace Wolff. I am a stonemason. I live in a small hamlet north of Anvil. One day months ago, I returned home after delivering a gargoyle to a customer in Stonebridge to find two Spirit Stalkers waiting. The undead messengers of evil wore black hooded cloaks, and were sitting motionless on huge steeds – black stallions with fiery red eyes, with my wife standing beside them in chains! In hissing voices they warned that unless I did their bidding, I would never see Luannah again. They took her away that day, and ever since I have been carving this block of granite. This morning the Spirit Stalkers returned and summoned a Warhawk to fly me to Yaztromo's Tower! My task was to put this keystone in place there, but as we flew southwest, I realized that Allansia would be doomed if I did. I stabbed the Warhawk's foot with my chisel, hoping to make it land. But it let go of the basket and I crashed to the ground. I know my injuries are fatal and I'll never see my wife again. But I had to do it to keep Allansia safe, at least until the Spirit Stalkers come calling for their keystone. Or should I say my tombstone.' The man chuckles briefly at his own dark humour, coughs and falls silent. You mop his fevered brow and ask him why Allansia is in danger. 'Bone. Zanbar Bone. His tower was once destroyed, and he with it, forever it was thought, but I know differently. The second coming of Bone is nigh. His loyal servant, Lord Azzur of Port Blacksand, has been plotting his return. Using arcane magic to turn Yaztromo's Tower black, and when this keystone is in place, the tower will itself summon Zanbar Bone to return from his twilight existence on the Demon Plain to rule Allansia.' Hakasan asks for more information about the man called Zanbar Bone. In an angry voice he replies, 'Man? Did I say Zanbar Bone is a man? Zanbar Bone is not a man, nor anything resembling a man. He is undead. He is the Night Prince. You must stop Bone. You must warn Yaztromo. You must get help from Nicodemus. You must rescue my wife, Luannah. You must. . .' But before he can finish his sentence, the stonemason's mouth falls open and his eyes widen into a fixed stare. His body stiffens as he sucks in his last gasp of air, exhaling slowly before slumping back down on the ground. 'The poor man. What a terrible curse put upon him. And what of Lord Azzur and Zanbar Bone? What does this all mean? Are we doomed? Or was he just delirious after the fall?' Hakasan asks. If you want to reply that you believe Horace's story, turn to **238**. If you want to reply that you believe he was delirious and speaking nonsense, turn to **190**.

368

The grass-covered foothills are easy enough to climb, but the going gets harder when the incline becomes steeper, and you have to avoid loose rocks and stones. Each hilltop you reach, you look eastwards hoping to catch sight of Skull Crag. Finally you see what you are looking for in the distance. It's a hill which stands above all others and, more importantly, it has a rounded top which resembles a human skull. Spurred on by the sighting, you scramble down the hill and press on. It's not long before you arrive at the entrance to a small cave at the foot of the next hill, which is still quite some distance away from Skull Crag. If you want to look inside the cave, turn to **265**. If you would rather keep heading east, turn to **236**.

369

You are not certain which way you are headed since you can't see the sun to get your bearings. Lose 1 *LUCK* point. If you want to keep going in the same direction, turn to **233**. If you want to go further right, turn to **293**.

370

You walk down the narrow tunnel for thirty metres, the light from your lantern casting eerie shadows against the rock wall. Suddenly you hear a dull rumbling sound coming from behind you. Turn to **157**.

Palace Street is lined with the grand houses of rich merchants and city officials, and leads into Palace Square, a picturesque tree-lined open space with flower beds and iron benches which seems strangely out of place with the rest of Port Blacksand's grim and dangerous districts. But the square was built for the enjoyment of one man for whenever he looked out from his residence you see opposite – the Palace of Lord Azzur. The imposing main building has two wings with a tall tower on both, from which the flag of Azzur flies. There are guards everywhere, but there is no sign of the two guards who absconded with Nicodemus. Suddenly a trumpet sounds loudly, a shrill call to the guards for them to stand to attention. The entrance gates open, and an opulent black-and-gold coach drawn by two black stallions drives out through the gates at speed, sliding sideways as it turns left in a cloud of dust, the coachman yelling at his steeds to go faster. You catch a glimpse of the passenger through the small window of the coach. It is somebody swathed in lavish navy blue robes with gold fastenings, his head completely wrapped in blue cloth held in place by jewelled brooches and his face totally hidden from view. It is the curse of Port Blacksand himself, Lord Azzur. The guards all stand frozen to the spot, not even daring to breathe as Lord Azzur drives by. With the entrance gates open, you realize you have the chance to enter the palace to find Nicodemus. The guard standing nearest to you on the corner of Palace Street is still standing to attention. If you want to knock him out and take his helmet and armour to enter the palace disguised as a guard, turn to **274**. If you want to walk into the palace as you are, turn to **353**.

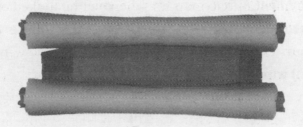

372

You search through the bandits' belongings and find two apples, a chunk of cheese wrapped in a damp cloth, a leather purse containing 2 Gold Pieces, a silver signet ring with a horseshoe engraving and a small stoppered glass bottle containing a purple-coloured liquid. You take the Gold Pieces and think about what else might be of use to you. Will you:

Eat the apple and cheese?	Turn to **266**
Try on the silver signet ring?	Turn to **141**
Drink the purple liquid?	Turn to **127**

373

You draw your sword and jump down. You land heavily on the ground, twisting your ankle. Lose 1 *SKILL* point and 1 *STAMINA* point. You do not have time to think before the slavering attack dogs pounce. Fight them one at a time.

	SKILL	STAMINA
First ATTACK DOG	6	6
Second ATTACK DOG	6	7

If you win, turn to **219**.

374

The bridge is narrow, forcing you to dismount and lead Stormheart on foot across it. You are almost halfway across when you hear the creaking sound of ropes straining on pulleys, as if pulled by invisible hands. The section of the flooring beneath your feet suddenly gives way, and you fall through the open trapdoor and land awkwardly with a splash in the cold water of Catfish River. Lose 1 *STAMINA* point and two items from your backpack. Stormheart gazes down through the open trapdoor, watching you drift downriver. You swim over to the north bank and climb out. You whistle to Stormheart to jump over the trapdoor on the bridge and trot over to you. Whilst you are drying yourself out, Stormheart drinks from the river and grazes on the lush grasses nearby. Annoyed by the unnecessary delay, you set off west again at a fast gallop, with the high city wall surrounding Port Blacksand just visible in the distance. The closer you get, the more you see of the dark rooftops and stark buildings jutting above the wall. You arrive an hour later at a small village of no more than a dozen thatch-roofed cottages just east of Port Blacksand. The villagers are weaving wicker baskets out of the long reeds that grow on the riverbank to sell them in the market in Port Blacksand. They stare at you as you pass by, in awe of your noble stallion. You are greeted by a smiling lady standing on her porch in front of a stack of wicker baskets. She is wearing a brightly coloured headscarf and a white apron over her long dress. 'Welcome to Flax,' she says in a jolly voice. 'My name's Cris. How can I help you?' You reply, saying you are on your way to Port Blacksand, whereupon her eyebrows rise in mild surprise. 'The thieves there will be pleased to see you. They love taking money from people of your ilk, all la-di-da on your big horse! If I were you, I'd hire a boat from my husband and row downriver and slip into Port Blacksand unnoticed. We can look after your horse while you're gone.' If you want to hire a boat to row to Port Blacksand, turn to **41**. If you want to turn down her offer and ride to the main city gates on Stormheart, turn to **264**.

375

A search of the cave yields nothing more than an old clay pot with a cracked lid. If you want to look inside the pot, turn to **51**. If you would rather leave the cave and press on towards Skull Crag, turn to **236**.

376

You lift the lid of the wooden chest and see that it is filled with lots of wooden boxes, all with the same ornately carved lid featuring a beetle motif identical to the one you found. You are convinced you have found Gurnard Jaggle's home, and the hot soup on the stove suggests to you that he is still very much alive. Hakasan agrees, saying, 'Maybe we should wait here until he returns?' If you want to wait for Gurnard Jaggle to appear, turn to **280**. If you would rather leave the tree house and carry on towards Yaztromo's Tower, turn to **251**.

377

You place your swords and backpacks on the ground, and as you turn to walk away, you hear the twang of bowstrings being released, and the whistle of arrows flying through the air. Roll one die. This is the number of arrows that strike you, with the minimum number being two. Lose 2 *STAMINA* points for each arrow that finds its mark. If you are still alive, turn to **76**.

378

The one-armed beggar looks at you quizzically and says, 'Did you say Gurnard Jaggle? I do know him. He was quite a character, was old Gurnard. He loved gold. For years he panned for gold in rivers and streams but didn't find a single nugget. He had a brief stint as a gold miner with the same result. Then he tried treasure hunting and mostly failed at that. He once found a small treasure chest in a cave but was robbed of the gold on his way back home. This made him angry, and he became very jealous of people who did find gold. One day he went a bit mad and started making booby-trapped boxes, placing them in caves and dungeons where treasure hunters might go searching. They say one unlucky adventurer died an untimely death after opening one of Gurnard's boxes. A friend of mine told me that Gurnard left Chalice a few months ago with a sackful of his deadly boxes and was never seen again, and is presumed dead. Beware of any wooden box you find with ornately carved lids and a beetle motif in the middle. It's likely to be one of Gurnard's specials!' You thank him for the information. If you want to show your map to the beggars, turn to **13**. If you would rather wish them well and walk on, turn to **311**.

The mention of Zanbar Bone turns Luannah's sadness into anger, and she starts cursing his name, blaming him for her husband's death before falling silent again. You row on in silence, with everybody lost in their own thoughts. Suddenly a large crow swoops down and lands on the bow of the boat, cawing loudly. 'Hello, Vermithrax. How are you?' Nicodemus says calmly. 'Fine, thanks,' the crow squawks in reply. You are surprised to hear the crow speaking perfect Allansian. Nicodemus explains that Vermithrax is Yaztromo's companion, named after his mentor, the archmage Vermithrax Moonchaser. 'And how is Yaztromo?' continues Nicodemus. 'Not so good,' the crow replies with its head tilted to one side. 'Yaztromo sent me here to tell you that the outside walls of his tower are now black from the ground all the way up to the fourth floor, and he predicts his tower will be completely black by tomorrow. A Warhawk landed on top of the tower this morning carrying the black keystone which it put in place on the edge of the parapet. Yaztromo is distraught that he was unable to move it. The final piece of bad news is that Skeletons have been gathering in Darkwood Forest, and are now moving slowly towards the Tower.' Nicodemus tells Vermithrax to tell Yaztromo that help is on its way. The crow squawks and flies off east. 'In the morning when the tower turns black, Zanbar Bone will return. The sorcery that destroyed him when he was a Night Prince would fail if he returns as a Demon Prince. How are we going to defeat him?' Nicodemus says, as though talking to himself, ruefully tapping his fingers on the side of the boat. 'If only I still had my special ring.' If you have the Ring of Burning Snakes in your possession, turn to **6**. If you do not have the ring, turn to **309**.

380

It is a finely crafted chain-mail coat and it fits you perfectly. Add 1 *SKILL* point. Pleased with your find, you walk on. Turn to **69**.

381

Hakasan looks sad, and says, 'Why did you say you were his enemy? His voice sounded quite friendly to me. Don't you think we should have spoken to him first? He might have been able to help us. Why was he calling out the name Bigleg? I wonder who he is. I guess we'll never know. We must bury him quickly and hurry on to Yaztromo's.' Turn to **246**.

382

Poking through the innards of the Lavaworm with the tip of your sword, you find a copper necklace with a circular copper name tag with the initials *MG* etched on it lying in the pool of green slime – no doubt the initials of some poor soul who came to the caves in search of gold but ended up as food for the Lavaworm. If you want to wear the necklace, turn to **57**. If you would rather leave it where it is and inspect the iron chest, turn to **212**.

383

You reach a section of the forest where the trees are closely packed together, making it difficult to see very far ahead. You walk on and almost stumble into a rope ladder which is suspended from an old oak tree. You look up to see that the rope ladder is hanging down from an open hatch of a large wooden tree house. You call out but there is no reply. You step warily on to the rope ladder and climb slowly up through the open trapdoor. You find yourself in a square room which serves as an all-in-one living room, bedroom and kitchen. There is nobody at home and you give the all-clear sign for Hakasan to climb up the rope ladder to join you. There is a wooden bed covered with animal furs in the corner of the far right-hand wall in front of which stands a large wooden chest with a beetle carving on the lid. A pan of vegetable soup is simmering on top of a small wood-burning stove. In the centre of the room there are two chairs tucked under a table, which has a candle glued to a skull welded to the table by thick lines of melted wax. Shelves fixed to the right-hand wall are lined with old leather-bound books kept upright by more animal skulls used as bookends. You cannot help but notice an unpleasant smell like rotten cabbage filling the room. Will you:

Drink the soup?	Turn to **84**
Look at the books?	Turn to **331**
Open the wooden chest?	Turn to **376**

If you don't want to stay in the tree house and would rather leave to continue your journey to Yaztromo's Tower, turn to **251**.

Shelves behind the shop counter are filled with gauntlets, helmets, axes, daggers and arrows, and the walls are covered with shields. Plate and chain-mail suits of armour stand against the right-hand wall. There is a glass case standing on the left side of the counter in which a magnificent sword is displayed, probably the finest you have ever seen in your life. The wide doorway behind the counter has a chain-mail curtain which is suddenly pushed aside by a hairy hand the size of a large ham. An enormous one-eyed creature steps through the curtains to stand behind the counter, leaning on it with its massive hands. 'Can I help you?' the CYCLOPS says with a smile, revealing a row of sharp spiked teeth. You point at the display case and ask if the sword is for sale. 'I'm sorry, this One-Eye is sold and awaiting collection. I could put you down for a new one if you would like to leave a deposit of 25 Gold Pieces? It should be ready in about three years. If that is too long for you to wait, might I suggest you buy one of my Demon Daggers for 10 Gold Pieces?' Will you:

Buy a Demon Dagger?	Turn to **195**
Attack the Cyclops to get the sword?	Turn to **171**
Leave the shop and walk to the end of Armoury Lane?	Turn to **33**

385

You see a well-worn studded leather gauntlet nestling in the undergrowth to the left of the path. It is damp and covered with mildew. If you want to try it on, turn to **270**. If you would rather leave it where it is and carry on, turn to **146**.

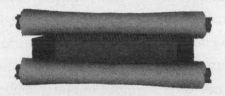

386

The howling gale is relentless and builds into a violent storm. The *Blue Marlin* struggles to climb each mountainous wave before surfing down the other side and crashing into the waiting trough. It is impossible to make good headway under sail, even with Mungo pulling hard on the tiller to keep his boat on course. You frantically bail water out of the boat with a bucket, but realize you are fighting a losing battle. Suddenly an enormous rogue wave crashes down on to the decks, sweeping you off your feet and washing you overboard into the sea. You can only watch helplessly as the *Blue Marlin* sails on, riding the giant waves of the storm. There is nothing Mungo can do to steer back to you, and once out of view, there is little hope of survival. Your adventure is over.

387

Making her escape, the girl snakes her way quickly through the crowded market. You run after her and grab her arm. She spins around, glaring at you fiercely, and manages to wriggle free. You calmly tell the girl to give you the pouch and that will be the end of the matter. She spits at you and slides her hand inside her smock to pull a knife from a hidden sheath. Seeing her move, you grab her wrist and take her knife from her, telling her to give you the pouch. 'Help!' she screams at the top of her voice. 'Help! I'm being robbed!' A crowd of people quickly gathers around you, several of them with daggers drawn. You try to protest your innocence, but with a knife in your hand, the crowd is having none of it. Nobody knows who you are. *Test Your Luck*. If you are Lucky, turn to **88**. If you are Unlucky, turn to **343**.

388

You feel very weak after your combat with the Scorpion Bug, and stand hunched over with your hands resting on your knees, panting heavily, deciding what to do next. Not wishing to go back to Hakasan empty-handed, you decide to go back to the tree house in the hope of finding something useful. It is late afternoon by the time you finally find it, but at least you get there without any further incidents. You climb up the rope ladder and look around the room.

You see that there is a drawer in the table which you hadn't noticed earlier, and pull it open to find a small wooden box with a plain lid. You shake the box and hear something rattling inside. If you want to open the box, turn to **161**. If you would rather leave it in the drawer and look for something else, turn to **189**.

389

You place the box in your backpack and walk over to the back of the cave, which you see is a dead end. You realize you have no option but to retrace your steps back to the outside world. You cross the cave floor and head back along the tunnel you came down. You soon arrive at a junction. If you want to go left, turn to **177**. If you want to go straight on, turn to **316**.

390

'Not so fast,' one of the Trolls says in a threatening tone, barring your way. 'Nobody enters the palace carrying weapons. Give them to me, and let Stinkfoot look inside your backpack.' The Troll called Stinkfoot grips your sword arm with an enormous green hand and says gruffly, 'Don't get any funny ideas. Just hand Twoteeth your sword nice and easy like.' If you want to comply with their demands, turn to **192**. If you want to try bribing the Trolls, turn to **5**.

391

You find a small cloth bag nailed to the underside of one of the wooden steps. It contains a copper bracelet which has mysterious runes etched on it. If you want to put the bracelet on, turn to **85**. If you would rather leave it behind and set off again for Moonstone Hills, turn to **164**.

392

The helmet once belonged to a Wood Elf noble and was forged with the finest steel. It fits on your head perfectly. Add 1 *SKILL* point. A search of the leather armour yields 10 Gold Pieces and a large sparkling ruby tucked away inside a secret pocket. Add 1 *LUCK* point. Pleased with your haul, you leave the idol to continue your quest to find Yaztromo. Turn to **284**.

393

The boots were taken by a Dwarf many years ago from the body of a High Elf who died at the hands of a Shapechanger in Darkwood Forest. The Dwarf used them as payment for food and lodgings at the farmhouse, where they were put in a box and forgotten about. Despite their worn-out appearance, the boots are incredibly comfortable and have magic properties. You have found a pair of elven boots. Add 1 *SKILL* point and 1 *LUCK* point. Turn to **98**.

394

The massive boulder thunders past you and crashes into the stream, causing a huge splash of water. You scramble behind cover and look up to see two sinewy men with long straggly hair and beards standing at the top of the hill shaking their fists. They are wearing animal skins, and they are both carrying a leather bag and a quiver of arrows across their shoulders. The WILD HILL MEN reach for their bows and fire two arrows down at you. *Test Your Luck*. If you are Lucky, turn to **55**. If you are Unlucky, turn to **140**.

395

You pull on the oars to send the small wooden boat on its way, gliding silently downstream towards the infamous city. Catfish River runs through the middle of Port Blacksand, and you see that the city wall arches over the river to allow small river craft to pass beneath it. As you go under the arch, the river turns noticeably darker and has an unpleasant smell, polluted by rubbish and sewage dumped in it. You need no reminding of the dangers that lurk inside the city, which is run with an iron fist by Lord Azzur and his Imperial Guards, who bleed payment from all who live here. It is known as the City of Thieves for good reason, being the main port of call for every pirate and freebooter in the Western Ocean, and home to Allansia's most notorious thieves and robbers. The first landmark you see from your boat is the high wall surrounding Lord Azzur's palace. On the opposite bank, two rowing boats are tied to an iron ring on a mooring on Axeman's Street, which leads up to Executioner's Square. Passing under Palace Bridge and Middle Bridge, you see plenty of seedy-looking characters busily going about their daily life. People are shouting at each other, and others are fighting. You hear dogs barking loudly, and the occasional shout for help, giving the port an air of dark foreboding. You pass under a third bridge, which is in a bad state of repair. It is lined with skulls on spiked poles, both human and non-human, which make eerie whistling sounds when the wind blows through them. You see a small hut underneath the bridge with steps leading down to it from above, and deduce it must be the fabled Singing Bridge where Nicodemus lives. Seeing nowhere to land your boat here, you carry on rowing, passing a row of dilapidated fishermen's cottages where women sit outside chatting, mending nets and gutting fish. At last you see the Black Lobster Tavern on the corner of Harbour Street and Lobster Wharf where the river meets the sea. The river is choppy here, and you have to row hard to reach the quay and moor up. There are three sailing ships docked in the harbour, one of them a pirate ship flying a black flag with the skull and crossbones. You jump out of the boat and walk up the ramp to where an ugly bunch of seamen and henchmen are standing. You try to push past them, but a bearded man in a black hat shouts, 'Grab that scurvy rat. We need another galley slave for the *Flying Toucan*.' If you hold a merchant's pass, turn to **149**. If you do not have this pass, turn to **357**.

396

You take the gold charm out of your pocket and hand it to the jeweller. He inspects it very carefully under a large magnifying glass, and says, 'This is a lovely little charm, the type which may have magical properties. I'm surprised you want to sell it. It's the sort of thing old Gurnard Jaggle was always searching for but never found! I'll give you 10 Gold Pieces for it.' If you want to accept his offer, turn to **214**. If you would rather say no to his offer and leave the jeweller's to walk to the end of the street, turn to **82**.

397

You cleave your sword through the thin membrane of the Sporeball like a knife through butter, splitting it in two. You are immediately consumed by a cloud of spore-filled dust, and breathe some of it in, which makes you cough violently. You drop to your knees, clutching your throat, with your lungs feeling like they are on fire. Inhaling these spores is lethal and there is nothing you can do to stop yourself from suffocating. The Sporeball has found a new host for its spores to grow into fungal parasites. Your adventure is over.

You run through the tall grasses without stopping until you can run no further. Lose 1 *STAMINA* point. You are exhausted and have to stop to get your breath back. You take a slug of water and set off again, scanning the horizon for the elusive Chaos Warrior, but don't see anybody who looks remotely like him. You keep thinking about Hakasan, who you left injured and alone in Darkwood Forest, wondering if she is safe. It's mid-afternoon by the time you arrive at Largo, a small village on the banks of Catfish River west of Darkwood Forest. The villagers are friendly river folk, who spend their days ferrying people and goods up and down Catfish River on their flat-bottomed boats. You walk round the village asking everybody you meet if they have seen a Chaos Warrior in the vicinity. The replies are negative until one very tall and stocky man by the name of Onx tells you that his cousin was paid 5 Gold Pieces to take a Chaos Warrior to Port Blacksand earlier in the day. 'My cousin was too frightened to say no to him. I can ferry you to Port Blacksand for 2 Gold Pieces if you wish?' the boatman says in a friendly voice. If you want to accept his offer, turn to **303**. If you would rather decline his offer and head back to find Hakasan, turn to **9**.

You look up at the hole and suddenly feel something cold and wet land on your face. It's not water but a jelly-like substance which begins to burn your skin. Lose 2 *STAMINA* points. You step away from under the hole as another globule drips down on to the floor with a dull plop. You hurriedly pour water from your flask over your face to wash off the flesh-eating green slime as a gelatinous blob appears in the hole in the ceiling. Turn to **174**.

Before settling down to enjoy Yaztromo's hospitality, the old wizard asks you to help him to remove the Demon's keystone that blights the roof of his tower. You climb the staircase on to the roof, where all four of you use your combined strength to push the black stone to the edge of the parapet. With one mighty heave, you push it over the edge, watching it fall to the ground and break up on the rocks below. Almost immediately the creepers engulfing Yaztromo's Tower start to wither and the walls of the tower start to lighten in colour. 'This is indeed a day for celebration,' Yaztromo says cheerfully. 'Can I have your attention, please? I have an important announcement to make. I have cakes!' With that, everybody rushes downstairs to sit at the dining table to enjoy the wide selection of delicious cakes. The two wizards have not seen each other in years, and spend as much time talking as eating. By his third cake, Nicodemus is yawning a lot, and says that he feels completely drained. Yaztromo tells him he can stay at his tower for as long as likes until he recovers his strength. Yaztromo asks you where you intend to go next in search of gold and glory. Without waiting for your reply, Hakasan says, 'Maybe we should try our luck in Fang? There is a purse of 10,000 Gold Pieces to be won in Baron Sukhumvit's Trial of Champions. It should be easy after this!' You remind her that only one person is allowed to come out of Sukhumvit's dungeon alive. 'That will be me, then!' she says cheekily. Everybody laughs and raises their glass in a toast to your next adventure, wherever it may take you. Yaztromo smiles warmly, and with his glass raised, looks you in the eye and says, 'Thank you for saving my tower. And thank you from all of us for saving Allansia. Maybe you should go back to Port Blacksand to tell Lord Azzur the good news. I'm sure he'd be delighted to see you! Whatever you choose to do, good *LUCK* on your adventure, and may your *STAMINA* never fail!'

HOW TO FIGHT
THE CREATURES OF
THE PORT OF PERIL

SKILL, STAMINA AND LUCK

To determine your *initial SKILL*, *STAMINA* and *LUCK* scores:

- Roll one die. Add 6 to this number and enter this total in the *SKILL* box on the Adventure Sheet.
- Roll both dice. Add 12 to the number rolled and enter this total in the *STAMINA* box.
- Roll one die, add 6 to this number and enter this total in the *LUCK* box.

SKILL reflects your swordsmanship and fighting expertise; the higher the better. *STAMINA* represents your strength; the higher your *STAMINA*, the longer you will survive. *LUCK* represents how lucky a person you are. Luck – and magic – are facts of life in the fantasy world you are about to explore.

SKILL, *STAMINA* and *LUCK* scores change constantly during an adventure, so keep an eraser handy. You must keep an accurate record of these scores. But never rub out your *initial scores*. Although you may receive additional

SKILL, *STAMINA* and *LUCK* points, these totals may never exceed your *initial* scores, except on very rare occasions, when instructed on a particular page.

BATTLES

When you are told to fight a creature, you must resolve the battle as described below. First record the creature's *SKILL* and *STAMINA* scores (as given on the page) in an empty *Monster Encounter Box* on your Adventure Sheet. The sequence of combat is then:

1. Roll the two dice for the creature. Add its *SKILL* score. This total is its Attack Strength.

2. Roll the two dice for yourself. Add your current *SKILL*. This total is your Attack Strength.

3. Whose Attack Strength is higher? If your Attack Strength is higher, you have wounded the creature. If the creature's Attack Strength is higher, it has wounded you. (If both are the same, you have both missed – start the next Attack Round from step 1 above.)

4. If you wounded the creature, subtract 2 points from its *STAMINA* score. You may use *LUCK* here to do additional damage (see "Using Luck in Battles" below).

5. If the creature wounded you, subtract 2 points from your *STAMINA* score. You may use *LUCK* to minimize the damage (see below).

6. Make the appropriate changes to either the creature's or your own *STAMINA* scores (and your *LUCK* score if you used *LUCK*) and begin the next Attack Round (repeat steps 1–6).

7. This continues until the *STAMINA* score of either you or the creature you are fighting has been reduced to zero (death).

LUCK

Sometimes you will be told to *Test Your Luck*. As you will discover, using *LUCK* is a risky business. The way you *Test Your Luck* is as follows:

Roll two dice. If the number rolled is equal to or less than your current *LUCK* score, you have been *Lucky*. If the number rolled is higher than your current *LUCK* score, you have been *Unlucky*. The consequences of being *Lucky* or *Unlucky* will be found on the page. Each time you *Test Your Luck,* you must subtract one point from your current *LUCK* score. So the more you rely on luck, the more risky this becomes.

USING LUCK IN BATTLES

In battles, you always have the option of using your *LUCK* either to score a more serious wound on a creature, or to minimize the effects of a wound the creature has just scored on you.

IF YOU HAVE JUST WOUNDED THE CREATURE: you may *Test Your Luck* as described below. If you are *Lucky*, subtract an extra 2 points from the creature's *STAMINA* score (i.e., 4 instead of 2 normally). But if you are *Unlucky*, you must restore 1 point to the creature's *STAMINA* (so instead of scoring the normal 2 points of damage, you have now only scored 1).

IF THE CREATURE HAS JUST WOUNDED YOU: you can *Test Your Luck* to try to minimize the wound. If you are lucky, restore 1 point of your *STAMINA* (i.e., instead of doing 2 points of damage, it has done only 1). If you are unlucky, subtract 1 extra *STAMINA* point.

Don't forget to subtract 1 point from your *LUCK* score each time you *Test Your Luck*.

RESTORING SKILL, STAMINA AND LUCK

SKILL

Occasionally, a page may give instructions to alter your skill score. A Magic Weapon may increase your *SKILL*, but remember that only one weapon can be used at a time!

You cannot claim 2 *SKILL* bonuses for carrying two Magic Swords. Your *SKILL* score can never exceed its *initial* value unless specifically instructed. Drinking the Potion of Skill (see later) will restore your *SKILL* to its initial level at any time.

STAMINA AND PROVISIONS

Your *STAMINA* score will change a lot during the adventure. As you near your goal, your *STAMINA* level may become dangerously low and battles may be particularly risky, so be careful!

You start the game with enough Provisions for ten meals. A separate *Provisions Remaining* box is provided on the Adventure Sheet for recording details of Provisions. You may eat only *one* meal at a time. When you eat a meal, add 4 points to your *STAMINA* score and deduct 1 point from your Provisions. Remember that you have a long way to go, so use your Provisions wisely!

Don't forget that your *STAMINA* score many never exceed its *initial* value unless specifically instructed on a page. Drinking the Potion of Strength (see later) will restore your *STAMINA* to its *initial* level at any time.

LUCK

You will find additions to your *LUCK* score awarded when you have been particularly *Lucky*. Remember that, as with *SKILL* and *STAMINA*, your *LUCK* score may never exceed its *initial* value unless specifically instructed on a page. Drinking the Potion of Fortune (see later) will restore your *LUCK* to its *initial* level at any time, and increase your *initial* luck by 1 point.

EQUIPMENT AND POTIONS

You start your adventure with a sword, leather armour, a shield and a backpack containing Provisions for the trip. But you will find lots more items as the adventure unfolds.

You may also take a magic potion which will aid you on your quest. Each bottle of potion contains enough for *one* measure; i.e., it can only be used *once* during an adventure. Choose ONE of the following:

- A Potion of Skill – restores *SKILL* points
- A Potion of Strength – restores *STAMINA* points
- A Potion of Fortune – restores *LUCK* points and adds 1 to *initial LUCK*

These potions may be taken at any time during the adventure. Taking a measure of potion will restore *SKILL*, *STAMINA* or *LUCK* scores to their *initial* level. The Potion of Fortune will increase your *initial LUCK* score by 1 point and restore *LUCK* to this new *initial* level.

HINTS ON PLAY

It will probably take you several attempts to make your way through *The Port of Peril*. Make notes and draw a map as you explore – this map will be useful in future adventures and help you identify unexplored areas.

Not all locations contain treasure; many merely contain traps and creatures. There are many "wild-goose chase" passages, and while you may progress through to your ultimate destination, it is by no means certain that you will win.

May the luck of the gods go with you on the adventure ahead!

ADVENTURE SHEET

SKILL

STAMINA

LUCK

EQUIPMENT

GOLD

TREASURE

PROVISIONS

MONSTER ENCOUNTERS

MONSTER: SKILL = STAMINA =	MONSTER: SKILL = STAMINA =
MONSTER: SKILL = STAMINA =	MONSTER: SKILL = STAMINA =
MONSTER: SKILL = STAMINA =	MONSTER: SKILL = STAMINA =
MONSTER: SKILL = STAMINA =	MONSTER: SKILL = STAMINA =
MONSTER: SKILL STAMINA =	MONSTER: SKILL STAMINA =
MONSTER: SKILL = STAMINA =	MONSTER: SKILL = STAMINA =

ADVENTURE SHEET

SKILL

STAMINA

LUCK

EQUIPMENT

GOLD

TREASURE

PROVISIONS

MONSTER ENCOUNTERS

MONSTER:
SKILL =
STAMINA =

MONSTER:
SKILL =
STAMINA =

MONSTER:
SKILL =
STAMINA =

MONSTER:
SKILL =
STAMINA =

MONSTER:
SKILL =
STAMINA =

MONSTER:
SKILL =
STAMINA =

MONSTER:
SKILL =
STAMINA =

MONSTER:
SKILL =
STAMINA =

MONSTER:
SKILL =
STAMINA =

MONSTER:
SKILL =
STAMINA =

MONSTER:
SKILL =
STAMINA =

MONSTER:
SKILL =
STAMINA =

YOU ARE **FIGHTING FANTASY** THE HERO

COLLECT THEM ALL, BRAVE ADVENTURER!

THE **WARLOCK** OF **FIRETOP MOUNTAIN**
STEVE JACKSON & IAN LIVINGSTONE

CITY OF **THIEVES**
IAN LIVINGSTONE

THE **CITADEL** OF **CHAOS**
STEVE JACKSON

THE **FOREST** OF **DOOM**
IAN LIVINGSTONE

HOUSE OF **HELL**
STEVE JACKSON

THE **PORT** OF **PERIL**
IAN LIVINGSTONE